Algy did not smile. 'Stop fooli[...]
he said curtly.

Bertie threw a glance at Ginger and came in.

'I wasn't going to mention this to you, Bertie, but as you're here you might as well listen to what I have to say,' resumed Algy.

'Go ahead,' said Ginger impatiently. 'What's on your mind?'

'I'm very much afraid that something serious has happened to Biggles.'

There was silence while the clock on the mantelpiece ticked out ten seconds and threw them into the past.

'Is this - official?' asked Ginger.

'No'

'Then what put the idea into your head?'

'This,' answered Algy, picking up a flimsy, buff-coloured slip of paper that lay on his desk. 'I'm promoted to Squadron Leader with effect from to-day, and . . . I am now in command of this squadron.'

Captain W. E. Johns was born in Hertfordshire in 1893. He flew with the Royal Flying Corps in the First World War and made a daring escape from a German prison camp in 1918. Between the wars he edited *Flying* and *Popular Flying* and became a writer for the Ministry of Defence. The first Biggles story, *Biggles the Camels are Coming* was published in 1932, and W. E. Johns went on to write a staggering 102 Biggles titles before his death in 1968.

www.kidsatrandomhouse.co.uk

BIGGLES BOOKS
PUBLISHED IN THIS EDITION

BIGGLES
FAILS to RETURN

CAPTAIN W.E. JOHNS

RED FOX

Red Fox would like to express their grateful thanks
for help given in the preparation of these editions to Jennifer Schofield,
author of *By Jove, Biggles*, Linda Shaughnessy of A. P. Watt Ltd
and especially to the late John Trendler.

BIGGLES FAILS TO RETURN
A RED FOX BOOK 0 09 993850 2

First published in Great Britain by Hodder and Stoughton 1943

This Red Fox edition published 2003

3 5 7 9 10 8 6 4 2 *IES*

Copyright © W E Johns (Publications) Ltd, 1943

Papers used by Random House Children's Books are natural, recyclable products
made from wood grown in sustainable forests. The manufacturing processes
conform to the environmental regulations of the country of origin.

Red Fox Books are published by Random House Children's Books,
61–63 Uxbridge Road, London W5 5SA,
a division of The Random House Group Ltd,
in Australia by Random House Australia (Pty) Ltd,
20 Alfred Street, Milsons Point, Sydney, NSW 2061, Australia,
in New Zealand by Random House New Zealand Ltd,
18 Poland Road, Glenfield, Auckland 10, New Zealand,
and in South Africa by Random House (Pty) Ltd,
Endulini, 5A Jubilee Road, Parktown 2193, South Africa

THE RANDOM HOUSE GROUP Limited Reg. No. 954009

A CIP catalogue record for this book is available from the British Library.

Printed and bound in Great Britain by
Cox & Wyman Ltd, Reading, Berkshire

Contents

Contents

Chapter 1
Where is Biggles?

Flight Lieutenant Algy Lacey, D.F.C., looked up as Flying Officer 'Ginger' Hebblethwaite entered the squadron office and saluted.

'Hello, Ginger—sit down,' invited Algy in a dull voice.

Ginger groped for a chair—groped because his eyes were on Algy's face. It was pale, and wore such an expression as he had never before seen on it.

'What's happened?' he asked wonderingly.

Before Algy could answer there was an interruption from the door. It was opened, and the effeminate face of Flight Lieutenant Lord 'Bertie' Lissie grinned a greeting into the room.

'What cheer, how goes it, and all that?' he murmured.

Algy did not smile. 'Stop fooling. Either come in or push off,' he said curtly.

Bertie threw a glance at Ginger and came in.

'I wasn't going to mention this to you, Bertie, but as you're here you might as well listen to what I have to say,' resumed Algy.

'Go ahead,' said Ginger impatiently. 'What's on your mind?'

'I'm very much afraid that something serious has happened to Biggles.'

There was silence while the clock on the mantelpiece ticked out ten seconds and threw them into the past.

'Is this—official?' asked Ginger.

'No.'

'Then what put the idea into your head?'

'This,' answered Algy, picking up a flimsy, buff-coloured slip of paper that lay on his desk. 'I'm promoted to Squadron Leader with effect from to-day, and . . . I am now in command of this squadron.'

'Which can only mean that Biggles isn't coming back?' breathed Ginger.

'That's how I figure it.'

'And you had no suspicion, before this order came in, that—'

'Yes and no,' broke in Algy. 'That is to say, I was not consciously alarmed, but as soon as I read that chit I knew that I had been uneasy in my mind for some days. Now, looking back, I can remember several things which make me wonder why I wasn't suspicious before.'

'But here, I say, you know, I thought Biggles was on leave?' put in Bertie, polishing his eyeglass briskly.

'So did we all,' returned Algy quietly. 'That, of course, is what we were intended to think.'

Bertie thrust his hands into his pockets. 'Biggles isn't the sort of chap to push off to another unit without letting us know what was in the wind,' he declared.

'Let us,' suggested Algy, 'consider the facts—as Biggles would say. Here they are, as I remember them, starting from the beginning. Last Thursday week Biggles had a phone call from the Air Ministry. There was nothing strange about that. I was in the office at the time and I thought nothing of it. When Biggles hung up he said to me—I remember his words distinctly—"Take care of things till I get back." I said "Okay." Of course, that has happened so many times

8

before that I supposed it was just routine. Biggles didn't get back that night till after dinner. He seemed sort of preoccupied, and I said to him, "Is everything all right?" He said, "Of course—why not?" ' Algy paused to light a cigarette with fingers that were trembling slightly.

'The next morning—that is, on the Friday—he surprised me by saying that he was taking the week-end off. I was surprised because, as you know, he rarely goes away. He has nowhere particular to go, and he has more than once told me that he would as soon be on the station as anywhere.'

'And you think this business starts from that time?' remarked Ginger.

'I'm sure of it. Biggles can be a pretty good actor when he likes, and there was nothing in his manner to suggest that anything serious was afoot. He tidied up his desk, and said he hoped to be back on Monday— that is, last Monday as ever was. We need have no doubt that when he said that he meant it. He *hoped* to be back. In other words, he would have been back last Monday if the thing—whatever it was—had gone off all right. When he went away he looked at me with that funny little smile of his and said, "Take care of things, old boy." Being rather slow in the uptake, I saw nothing significant about that at the time, but now I can see that it implied he was not sure that he was coming back.'

Ginger nodded. 'That fits in with how he behaved with me. Normally, he's a most undemonstrative bloke, but he shook hands with me and gave me a spot of fatherly advice. I wondered a bit at the time, but, like you, I didn't attach any particular importance to it.'

'It wasn't until after he'd gone,' continued Algy,

'that I discovered that he'd left the station without leaving an address or telephone number. Knowing what a stickler he is for regulations, it isn't like him to break them himself by going off without leaving word where he could be found in case of emergency. That was the last we've seen of him. I didn't think anything of it until Wednesday, when I had to ring up Forty Squadron. It was their guest night, and Biggles was to be guest of honour. He had accepted the invitation. Biggles doesn't accept invitations and then not turn up. When he accepted that one you can bet your life he intended to be there; and the fact that he didn't turn up, or even ring up, means that he couldn't make it. It must have been something serious to stop him. I began to wonder what he could be up to. Yesterday I was definitely worried, but when this Group order came in this morning, posting me to the command of the squadron, it hit me like a ton of bricks. To sum up, I suspect the Ministry asked Biggles to do a job, a job from which there was a good chance he wouldn't come back. He went. Whatever the job was, it came unstuck. He didn't get back. It takes a bit of swallowing, but there it is. It's no use blinking at facts, but the shock has rather knocked me off my pins. I thought you'd better know, but don't say anything to the others — yet.'

Ginger spoke. 'If the Air Ministry has given you the squadron they must *know* he isn't coming back.'

Algy nodded. 'I'm afraid you're right.'

Bertie stepped into the conversation. 'But that doesn't make sense — if you see what I mean? If the Ministry *knows* that something has happened to Biggles his name would be in the current casualty list — killed, missing, prisoner, or something.'

10

'That depends on what sort of job it was,' argued Algy. 'The Ministry might know the truth, but it might suit them to say nothing.'

'But that isn't good enough,' protested Ginger hotly. 'We can't let Biggles fade out . . . just like that.' He snapped his fingers.

'What can we do about it?'

'There's one man who'll know the facts.'

'You mean—Air Commodore Raymond, of Intelligence?'

'Yes.'

'He won't tell us anything.'

'Won't he, by thunder!' snorted Ginger. 'After all the sticky shows we've done for him, and the risks we've taken for his department, he can't treat us like this.'

'Are you going to tell him that?' asked Algy sarcastically.

'I certainly am.'

'But it's against orders to go direct to the Air Ministry—you know that.'

'Orders or no orders, I'm going to the Air House,' declared Ginger. 'They're glad enough to see us when they're stuck with something they can't untangle; they can't shut the door when they don't want to see us. Oh, no, they can't get away with that. I'm going to see the Air Commodore if I have to tear the place down brick by brick until I get to him. Is he a man or is he a skunk? I say, if he's a man he'll see us, and come clean.'

'You go on like this and we shall all finish under close arrest.'

'Who cares?' flaunted Ginger. 'I want to know the truth. If Biggles has been killed—well, that's that.

11

What I can't stand is this uncertainty, this knowing nothing. Dash it, it isn't fair on us.'

'I am inclined to agree with you,' said Algy grimly. 'Ours has been no ordinary combination, and Raymond knows that as well as anybody. Let's go and tackle the Air Commodore. He can only throw us out.'

'Here, I say, what about me?' inquired Bertie plaintively. 'Don't I get a look in?'

'Come with us, and we'll make a deputation of it,' decided Algy.

An hour later an Air Ministry messenger was showing them into an office through a door on which was painted in white letters the words, *Air Commodore R. B. Raymond, D.S.O. Air Intelligence*. The Air Commodore, who knew Algy and Ginger well, and had met Bertie, shook hands and invited them to be seated.

'You know, of course, that you had no business to come here on a personal matter without an invitation?' he chided gently, raising his eyebrows.

'This is more than a personal matter, sir,' answered Algy. 'It's a matter that concerns the morale of a squadron. You've probably guessed what it is?'

The Air Commodore nodded. 'I know. I was wondering how long you would be putting two and two together. Well, I'm very sorry, gentlemen, but there is little I can tell you.'

'Do you mean you can't or you won't, sir?' demanded Ginger bluntly.

'What exactly is it you want to know?'

Algy answered: 'Our question is, sir, where is Biggles?'

'I wish I knew,' returned the Air Commodore slowly, and with obvious sincerity.

'But you know where he went?'

'Yes.'

'Will you tell us that?'

'What useful purpose would it serve?'

'We might be able to do something about it.'

'I'm afraid that's quite out of the question.'

'Do you mean—he's been killed?'

'He may be. In fact, what evidence we have all points to that. But we have no official notification of it.'

There was a brief and rather embarrassing silence. The Air Commodore gazed through the window at the blue sky, drumming on his desk with his fingers.

'Knowing what we have been to each other in the past, sir, don't you think we are entitled to some explanation?' pressed Algy.

'The matter is secret.'

'So were a good many other things you've told us about in the past, sir, when you needed Biggles to straighten them out.'

The Air Commodore appeared to reach a decision. He looked round. 'Very well,' said he. 'Your argument is reasonable, and I won't attempt to deny it. I'll tell you what I know—in the strictest confidence, of course.'

'We've never let you down yet, sir,' reminded Algy.

'All right. Don't rub it in.' The Air Commodore smiled faintly, then became serious. 'Here are the facts. About ten days ago we received information that a very important person whom I need not name, but who I will call Princess X, had escaped from Italy. This lady is an Italian, or, rather, a Sicilian, one of those who hate Mussolini* and all his works. Her father, well

---

* Benito Mussolini—Fascist dictator of Italy. Joined with Germany in the war against Britain and her allies in 1940.

13

known before the war for his anti-Fascist views, was killed in what was alleged to be an accident. Actually he was murdered. Princess X knew that, and she plotted against the regime. Mussolini's police found out, and when Italy entered the war she was arrested. Friends— members of a secret society—inside Italy helped her to escape. She was to make for Marseilles, where we had made arrangements to pick her up. Unfortunately, she was pursued, and in the hope of eluding her pursuers she struck off at a tangent and eventually reached the Principality of Monaco, in the south-east corner of France, where she knew someone, a wealthy Italian business man, a banker, whom she had befriended in the past. She thought he would give her shelter. She reached his villa safely, and got word through to us by one of our agents who was in touch with her, giving us the address, and imploring us to rescue her. By this time the hue and cry was up, and it would have been suicidal for her to attempt to reach Marseilles, or a neutral country—Spain, for instance—alone. We were most anxious to have her here, and we realized that if anything was to be done there was no time to lose. We decided to attempt to rescue her by air. We sent for Bigglesworth, who has had a lot of experience at this sort of thing, and asked his opinion. He offered to do the job.'

'You mean, go to Monaco, pick up the princess and bring her here?'

'Yes. But the job was not as easy as it sounds—not that it sounds easy. The difficulty did not lie so much in getting Biggles there, because he could be dropped by parachute; but to pick him up was a different matter. That meant landing an aircraft. There is no landing ground in Monaco itself, which is nearly all rock, and

14

mostly built over as well. For that matter there are very few landing grounds in the Alpes Maritimes—the department of France in which Monaco is situated. It was obviously impossible for Biggles to fly the aircraft himself, because during the period while he would be fetching the princess—perhaps a matter of two or three days—the machine would be discovered. So we called in a man who knows every inch of the country, a man who was born there, a Monégasque* who is now serving with the Fighting French**. It was decided to drop Biggles by parachute and pick him up twenty-four hours later at a place suggested by this lad, whose name, by the way, is Henri Ducoste. Ducoste suggested a level area of beach just west of Nice, about twenty miles from Monaco, a spot that in pre-war days was used for joy-riding.'

'Why so far away?' asked Ginger.

'Because, apparently, there is nowhere nearer. Monaco is a tiny place. All told, it only covers eight square miles. Almost from the edge of the sea the cliffs rise steeply to a couple of thousand feet, and, except for a few impossible slopes, the whole principality is covered with villas and hotels. The fashionable resort, Monte Carlo, occupies most of it. The actual village of Old Monaco, and the palace, are built on a spur of rock. There is no aerodrome. In fact, there isn't an airport nearer than Cannes, some thirty miles to the west.'

'I understand, sir,' said Ginger.

* A native of Monaco.
** After France was occupied by the Germans, those members of the French forces who managed to escape set up a new headquarters in Britain led by General de Gaulle. They continued fighting from there and were known as the Fighting French or Free French.

The Air Commodore resumed. 'Well, Biggles went. Precisely what occurred in Monaco we don't know; it seems unlikely that we shall ever know, but as far as we have been able to deduce from the meagre scraps of information that our agents have collected, what happened was this. Biggles walked into a trap. The Princess was not at the villa. She had been betrayed by her supposed friend, presumably for the big reward that had been offered, and was in custody, in the civil prison, awaiting an escort to take her back to Italy. It seems that not only did Biggles extricate himself from the trap, but almost succeeded in what must have been the most desperate enterprise of his career. He rescued the Princess from the prison, and actually used· an Italian police car to make his getaway. In this car he and the Princess raced to Nice, using that formidable highway that cuts through the tops of the mountains overlooking the sea, known as the Grande Corniche. The car was followed, of course, but Biggles got to the landing ground just ahead of his pursuers. Ducoste was there, waiting. The moon made everything plain to see.' The Air Commodore paused to light a cigarette.

'The story now becomes tragic,' he continued. 'What I know I had from the lips of Ducoste. Biggles and the princess left the car and ran towards the aircraft, closely followed by the Italians. To enable you to follow the story closely I must tell you that the machine was an old Berline Breguet, a single-engined eight-seater formerly used by the Air France Company on their route between London and the Riviera. As a matter of detail, this particular machine was the one in which Ducoste made his escape from France. The decision to use it was his own. Between the cockpit and the cabin there is a bulkhead door with a small glass window in

16

it so that the pilot can see his passengers. I'm sorry to trouble you with these details, but, for reasons which you will appreciate in a moment, they are important. As I have said, Biggles and the princess, closely pursued, ran towards the machine. Ducoste, who was watching from the cockpit, with his engine ticking over, saw that it was going to be a close thing. Biggles shouted to the princess to get aboard and tried to hold the Italians with his pistol. We can picture the situation — the princess near the machine, with Biggles, a few yards behind, walking backwards, fighting a rearguard action. The princess got aboard, whereupon Biggles yelled to Ducoste to take off without him. Naturally, Ducoste, who does not lack courage, hesitated to do this. What I must makè clear is, the princess actually got aboard. Of that there is no doubt. Ducoste felt the machine move slightly, in the same way that one can feel a person getting into a motor-car. He looked back through the little glass window and saw the face of the princess within a few inches of his own. She appeared to be agitated, and made a signal which Ducoste took to mean that he was to take off. I may say that all this is perfectly clear in Ducoste's mind. He looked out and saw Biggles making a dash for the machine; but before Biggles could reach it he fell, apparently hit by a bullet. Ducoste, from his cockpit, could do nothing to help him. By this time bullets were hitting the machine, and in another moment they must all have been caught. In the circumstances he did the most sensible thing. He took off. Remember, there was no doubt in his mind about the princess being on board. He had actually seen her in the machine. He made for England, and after a bad journey, during which he was several times attacked by enemy fighters, he reached his base aerodrome. Judge his consternation when he found the cabin empty. The princess was not there. The cabin door was open. Poor Ducoste was incoherent with mortification and amazement. The last thing he saw before he took off was Biggles lying motionless on the ground, and two Italians within a dozen yards, running towards him. The last he saw of the princess she was in the machine.'

Algy drew a deep breath. 'And that's all you know?'

'That is all we know.'

'No word from Monaco?'

'Nothing.'

There was a brief silence.

'Ducoste has absolutely no idea of what happened to the princess?' asked Ginger.

'None whatever, although the obvious assumption is that she fell from the aircraft some time during the journey from the South of France to England. What else can we think?'

'No report of her body having been found?'

'Not a word.'

'What an incredible business,' muttered Algy. 'As far as Biggles is concerned, the Italians must know about him from their Nazi friends. One would have thought that had he been killed the enemy would have grabbed the chance of boasting of it—that's their usual way of doing things.'

'One would think so,' agreed the Air Commodore. 'But it seems certain that if he wasn't killed he must have been badly wounded, in which case he would have been captured, which comes to pretty much the same thing. But I don't overlook the possibility that it may have suited the enemy to say nothing about the end of a man who has given them so much trouble.

From every point of view it is a most unsatisfactory business.'

'Tell me, sir; how was Biggles dressed for this affair?' asked Ginger. 'Was he in uniform?'

'Well, he was and he wasn't. I know he has a prejudice against disguises, but this was an occasion when one was necessary. He could hardly walk about Monaco in a British uniform, so he wore over it an old blue boiler suit, which he thought would give him the appearance of a workman of the country.'

'And you don't expect to hear anything more, sir?'

'Frankly, no. There is just one hope—a remote one, I fear. I had a private arrangement with Biggles. Realizing that there was a chance of his picking up useful information which, in the event of failure, he would not be able to get home, he took with him a blue pencil, the idea being that we could profit by what he had learned should he fail, and should we decide to follow up with another agent. He said that should he be in Monaco he would write on the stone wall that backs the Quai de Plaisance, in the Condamine—that is, the lower part of Monaco in which the harbour is situated. If he were in Nice he would write on the wall near Jock's Bar, below the Promenade des Anglais. His signature would be a blue triangle.'

'Have you checked up to see if there is such a message?' queried Algy.

'No,' admitted the Air Commodore.

'Why not?'

'The place is swarming with police. In any case, there seemed to be no point in it, because whatever Biggles wrote before the rescue would be rendered valueless after what happened on the landing ground. Right up to the finish he must have hoped to get home, and after that time it seems unlikely to say the least that he would have an opportunity for writing.'

'But, sir,' put in Ginger, 'haven't you thought of trying to rescue Biggles?'

'I have, but it seemed hopeless.'

'Why? Nothing is ever hopeless.'

'But consider the circumstances. Biggles was last seen lying on the ground, dead or unconscious, right in front of his pursuers.'

'Yet you admit that if they had got him they would probably have issued a statement?'

'That doesn't necessarily follow.'

'Why should they withhold the information?'

'I could think of several reasons. The princess has friends in Italy, and Mussolini might fear repercussions, if it became known that she had been killed. Again the enemy might think that if they kept silent we should send more agents down to find out what happened, and thus they would catch more birds in the same trap. Neither side willingly tells the other anything, for which reason we have refrained from putting Biggles' name in the casualty list.'

'You don't hold out any hope for him?'

'How can I?'

'And the princess?'

'The chances of her survival seem even more remote. If she was not killed on the landing ground, then she certainly must have lost her life when she fell from the aircraft.'

Algy looked straight at the Air Commodore. 'I think it's about time somebody found out just what did happen, sir,' he said curtly.

'Absolutely—yes, by Jove—absolutely,' breathed Bertie.

'I'm sorry, but I have no one to send.'

'Then perhaps you would use your influence to get me ten days leave, sir?' suggested Algy meaningly.

The Air Commodore's expression did not change. 'Are you thinking of going to Monaco?'

'I shan't sleep at night until I know what happened to Biggles.'

'That goes for all of us, sir,' interposed Ginger.

'But be reasonable, you fellows,' protested the Air Commodore. 'I know exactly how you feel, but war isn't a personal matter . . .'

'You didn't take that view when you were trying to rescue the princess,' returned Algy shortly. 'Frankly, I don't care two hoots about her, because I've never seen her and I'm never likely to; but Biggles happens to be my best friend. Apart from which, he is one of the most valuable officers in the service. Surely it is worth going to some trouble to try to get him back—or at least, find out what happened to him?'

'I agree, but the chances of success are so small that they are hardly worth considering.'

'I am sorry, sir, but I can't agree with you there,' replied Algy bluntly. 'Until I know Biggles is dead I shall assume that he is alive. Get me ten days leave and I'll find out what happened to him.'

'Include me in that, sir,' put in Ginger.

'And me, sir,' murmured Bertie.

The Air Commodore looked from one to the other. 'Just what do you think you are going to do?'

Algy answered. 'I don't know, except that we are going to find out what happened to Biggles. If the thing was the other way round, do you suppose he'd be content to sit here knowing that we were stuck in enemy country? Not on your life!'

'It is my opinion that Biggles is dead,' asserted the Air Commodore.

'I had already sensed that, sir, but I don't believe it,' retorted Algy. 'Call it wishful thinking if you like, but I'll believe it when I've seen his body, not before.'

The Air Commodore shrugged his shoulders. 'All right,' he said crisply. 'Have it your own way. Think of a reasonable scheme and I'll consider it.'

Algy rose and picked up his cap. 'Thank you, sir. It is now twelve o'clock. We'll go and have some lunch, and be back here at two.'

The Air Commodore nodded. 'Very well.'

Chapter 2
The Reasonable Plan

Over lunch, and afterwards, in a secluded corner of the
Royal Air Force Club, in Piccadilly, Algy, Bertie and
Ginger, discussed the situation that had arisen. Neither
Algy nor Ginger had ever been to Monaco, so they
were somewhat handicapped; but it turned out that to
Bertie the celebrated little Principality was a sort of
home from home. For several years he had gone there
for the 'season' as a competitor in the international
motor car race called the Monte Carlo Rally. He had
competed in the motor-boat trials, had played tennis
on the famous courts, and golf on the links at Mont
Agel. He had stayed at most of the big hotels, and had
been a guest at many of the villas owned by leading
members of society. As a result, he not only knew the
principality intimately, but the country around it.

'Why didn't you tell the Air Commodore this?' asked
Algy.

'Never play your trump cards too soon—no, by Jove,'
murmured Bertie, and then went on to declare that if
only they could get to Monaco he knew of places where
they could hide.

'It seems to be taken for granted that we are all
going,' observed Algy.

Bertie and Ginger agreed—definitely.

'Then the first question we must settle is, how are
we going to get there?'

'There doesn't seem to be much choice,' Ginger

pointed out. 'Either we can land on this beach aerodrome near Nice, or we can bale out. But however we go down, someone will have to bring the machine back. We all want to stay there, so I suggest that we ask Raymond to lend us his Monégasque pilot—the bloke who flew Biggles. He must know the lie of the land a lot better than we shall find out from the map.'

'That's a good idea,' agreed Algy. 'Do we land or do we jump?'

'If this lad knows the country I'm in favour of landing,' declared Bertie. 'It's pretty rough for jumping—rocks and things all over the place.'

'All right. Let us say that we land,' went on Algy. 'Having landed, do we stay together or do we work separately?'

'I'm in favour of working separately,' said Ginger. 'That gives us three chances against one. If we stay together, and anything goes wrong, we all get captured. If everyone takes his own line we shall avoid that, and at the same time cover more ground. I propose that we work separately, but each knowing roughly what the others are going to do. We might have a rendezvous where we can get in touch and compare notes.'

'Yes, I think that's sound reasoning,' agreed Algy, and Bertie confirmed it. 'How are we going—I mean, we can't stroll about Monte Carlo in uniform? I speak French pretty well, so I could put on a suit of civvies and pretend to be a French prisoner of war just repatriated from Germany. That would account for my being out of touch with things. What about you, Bertie?'

'Well, I speak the jolly old lingo, and I know my way about. That ought to do.'

Algy looked doubtful. 'People may wonder what an

able-bodied chap like you is doing, strolling about with no particular job.'

'I'll take my guitar and be an out-of-work musician—how's that?' Bertie smiled at the expressions on the faces of the others. 'Strolling players are common in the South of France,' he explained. 'They make a living playing round the pub doors, and that sort of thing. By Jove, yes; I could do the jolly old Blondin act, playing a tune round the likely places, trusting that Biggles would recognize it if he were about. Biggles would know that piece I play with all the twiddly bits. He once told me he'd never forget it.'

Algy smiled. 'All right. What about you, Ginger?'

Ginger looked glum. 'My trouble is I can't speak French—or not enough to amount to anything. I can speak a bit, enough to make myself understood, but I couldn't pass as a Frenchman. I speak better Spanish. Before the war we spent more time in Spain, and Spanish America, than in France.'

'But we're not going to Spain. We're going to France,' Algy pointed out sarcastically.

'Just a minute though, I think I've got something,' put in Bertie. 'Yes, by jingo, that's it. Ginger can be a Spaniard.'

'Doing what?'

'Selling onions. In the same way those chappies from northern France used to come over to England with their little strings of onions, the lads from Spain surge along the Riviera selling the jolly old vegetable. Or if he likes he can be a bullfighter looking for work—they still have bull-fights in the South of France.'

'Not for me,' declared Ginger. 'I might be offered a job. I'll sell onions.'

'Where are you going to get the onions?' inquired Algy.

'Plenty on the aerodrome. You forget our lads have turned market gardeners.'

'Okay, then we'll call that settled. But we seem to have overlooked the most important thing of all. How are we going to get back?'

'By Jove, that's a nasty one,' muttered Bertie. 'I'd clean forgotten about the return tickets.'

'There's only one way,' asserted Ginger. 'Assuming that Ducoste will take us over, he'll have to pick us up again. We should have to fix a place and time. Naturally, we should all have to keep that date, whatever happened. If we don't locate Biggles, or find out what happened to him, in that time, the chances are that we never should. If we finish before that time we should just have to lie doggo until the plane came for us. We could flash a light signal to Ducoste to let him know that it was okay to land.'

'I can't think of anything better than that,' admitted Algy. 'Of course, if we made a mess of things we shouldn't be there, anyway, in which case Ducoste would push off again. We couldn't ask him to hang about. Anything else?'

'That seems to be about as far as we can get,' opined Ginger. 'When we get back to the aerodrome, are you going to let the others in on this?'

'No,' decided Algy. 'The whole squadron would want to come. We can't have that—the show would begin to look like a commando raid, or an invasion. Angus can take over while I'm away. Well, let's get along and put the proposition to the Air Commodore. We can fix the details later.'

'What details?' asked Ginger.

'We shall need French money, forged identity papers, and so on. Raymond will get those for us if he approves the scheme.'

'If he does, when are we going to start?'

'Obviously, just as soon as we are ready,' answered Algy. 'The sooner we are on the spot the better. We ought to be away by to-morrow night at latest.' He got up. 'Let's get back to the Ministry. I'm anxious to get this thing settled.'

Half an hour later he was laying the proposition before Commodore Raymond, who listened patiently until he had finished.

'You fellows are all old enough to know what you're doing,' said the Air Commodore quietly, at the conclusion. 'But for the fact that you have had experience in this sort of deadly work I wouldn't consider the project. However, your previous successful operations do entitle you to special consideration. I must say, though, that I shall be very much surprised if I see any of you again until the end of the war—if then. By discarding your uniforms you will become spies, in which case, it is hardly necessary for me to tell you, it is no use appealing to me if you are caught*. I'm sorry if that sounds discouraging, but we must face the facts. I'll make arrangements with your Group for you to go on leave, and supply you with such things as you think you will require, as far as it is in my power. I'll get in touch with Ducoste right away and tell him to telephone you at the squadron. He volunteered for the last show, and I have no doubt he'll do so again. He can

---

* Soldiers, who were captured by the enemy, were entitled to be humanely treated and held prisoner, but spies on both sides were shot, if captured. If a soldier wore disguise or discarded his uniform he was considered a spy and liable to be shot.

have the Breguet. It will be less likely to attract attention over France than one of our machines, and at the same time save us from using—I nearly said losing—one of ours. If he's caught he'll be shot, so don't let him down. Anything else?'

'Just one thing, sir,' requested Ginger. 'What is the name of the Italian businessman you mentioned, the fellow at whose villa the princess hoped to stay—the skunk who let her down?'

'The man is a retired Milanese banker named Zabani—Gaspard Zabani. His place is the Villa Valdora, in the Avenue Fleurie. Why did you ask that?'

'Since, apparently, he is well in with the Italian secret police, he may know how his betrayal of the princess ended. He might be induced to speak.'

A ghost of a smile crossed the Air Commodore's face. 'I see. As far as I'm concerned you can do what you like with him. He must be an exceptionally nasty piece of work. But while we are on the subject of the Italian secret police, be careful of a fellow named Gordino. He is in charge of things on the Riviera. He's a short, dark, stoutish, middle-aged man—usually wears a dark civilian suit. He's got an upturned black moustache and a scar on his chin. He looks rather like a prosperous little grocer, but don't be deceived by that. He's a cunning devil.'

'What a bounder the blighter must be,' murmured Bertie in his well-dressed voice.

'Matter of fact, he is,' agreed the Air Commodore, smiling. He stood up. 'And now, gentlemen, if that's all, I must ask you to be on your way. I've a pile of work in front of me. I'll get Henri Ducoste to ring you later.'

'Thank you, sir, for giving us so much of your time,'

said Algy. 'We are grateful to you for being frank and for giving us this chance. Biggles shall know about it—when we find him.'

'Bring Biggles back alive and I shall be amply repaid,' returned Air Commodore Raymond. 'Good luck to you.'

Still discussing the plan the deputation returned to the aerodrome.

At nine o'clock that night an officer in the uniform of the Fighting French Air Force walked into the ante-room. Ginger saw him first, and guessed at once who he was, although they had been expecting a phone call, not a personal appearance. Nudging Bertie, he went to meet the visitor.

'Henri Ducoste?' he queried.

Smiling, the French airman nodded assent. He was a slim, dark young man, with straight, rather long black hair, and a shy manner. Ginger had visualized—not that the Air Commodore had given any reason for it—an older man. He judged him to be not more than nineteen.

Having introduced himself and Bertie, Ginger took his arm, saying. 'Let's get out of the crowd.' They went to the station office where Algy was busy clearing up some squadron matters to leave everything shipshape for Angus to take over. Henri was introduced.

'I have spoken with your Air Commodore,' he said in fair English. 'Better than the telephone, I think I come here and talk.'

'Much better idea,' agreed Algy. 'Sit down. Cigarette? Did the Air Commodore tell you just what we had in mind?'

'Yes, he tells me all you know, I think.'

'You know we want you to fly us to Monaco?'

'But yes.'

'How do you feel about it?'

Henri shrugged his shoulders. 'How you say? Okay wiz me. I go anywhere. What does it matter?'

'That's the spirit,' returned Algy.

'Only with one thing I do not agree so much,' went on Henri, frankly.

'What's that?'

'I understand not quite this making of a landing at Californie, on the beach by Nice.'

'What's wrong with that?'

'*Tiens!* We have use it one time. The Italian mens are not of the most clever, but they are not always the fools. They stop any more landings at Nice, I think. Perhaps there may be now the trench, the wire, or the big sticks of wood, to make a crash.' Henri shrugged. 'I don't know, but it would be good to make sure.'

'By Jove, you know, the lad's right—absolutely right,' declared Bertie. 'No bally use busting ourselves right at the word go, or anything like that—if you see what I mean?'

'I see what you mean all right,' agreed Algy thoughtfully. 'It would be taking a pretty hefty risk to use this landing ground without first confirming that there were no obstructions. I always realized that, but I couldn't think of an alternative. Of course, once we were there we could check up, and if the place was all right we could use it to go home from.' To Henri he said, 'Can you think of a better plan?'

'There are two ways more,' announced Henri. 'Either we find another aerodrome or you use the parachute. There is no other aerodrome for many kilometres. *Alors!* I think it better to use the parachute.'

'That seems to be a sound argument,' agreed Algy,

'but I was given to understand that the country round Monaco was dangerous for parachute landings—rocks and ravines, and so on?'

'*Oui*. But there are places where the rocks are not too close. I live all my life at Monaco. I know such a place. It is much nearer to Monaco than Californie, only three, perhaps four, miles. *Regardez**. Here is my map. I show you.'

Henri unfolded his map on the desk. '*Voila!*' he continued. 'Here we have Monaco. There are three roads. One, she go east to Italy. Two, she go west to Nice, Cannes, and sometime to Marseilles. Three, she go north, very steeply up the mountain, to the village of La Turbie. Behind La Turbie a road the most small she goes to Peille. On the left of the road, we have a wide valley, many kilometres long. Men who make the farm in the valley, they clear away all the big rock. You jump there and you make only four miles down the mountain to Monaco. And there is another thing I tell you. From La Turbie to Monaco you need not the road use. On it perhaps there are the soldiers and the police. See here.' Henri pointed on the map to a more or less straight line that ran from La Turbie to Monaco. 'That is the old mountain railway—very steep, very dangerous. One day the train she go down the mountain alone. Zip! Many people they are killed, so the railway she runs no more. But the line is still there, and so when I was a boy we ascend to La Turbie by the iron rails. If you land in my valley you can go straight down the line into Monaco and no one knows—no one see you. How's that?'

* French: look.

'Pretty good,' agreed Algy. 'But about the parachutes. We have things to carry; they are likely to get broken.'

'We can heave them over on a special brolly*,' suggested Ginger.

'Yes, of course. But what shall we do with the parachutes, Henri? Is there any place where we can hide them?'

Again Henri stabbed the map with an enthusiastic finger. 'Here on the Peille road there are no 'ouses. Only one. The stone walls have all fall down. Put your parachutes inside and cover them with stones, and no one sees them. But it is so simple.'

Algy looked at the others. 'Henri has certainly got the right ideas. We'll take his advice.'

'I throw you down in good place,' promised Henri. 'I am a Monégasque. I know this country all over.' His eyes moistened, without shame, as only those of a Latin can. 'One day I go back and see my mother, and my little sister, Jeanette. My father, he is dead five years now.'

'And your mother still lives at Monaco?' asked Algy.

'But yes.'

'Where? It might be possible that we could give her a message from you.'

'*La-la?* That would be the most marvellous!' cried Henri. 'They know I go to the war and for them that is the end. They do not know if I am alive or dead. I dare not try to send the message, because if it is known I fly for De Gaulle perhaps they are put in a concentration camp for hostages.'

'Where do they live?'

---

* Slang: parachute.

'At Monaco, on the rock—the old village. Number six, Rue Marinière. It is the first little street opposite the palace. If you see them, say that Pepé'—Henri blushed slightly—'they call me Pepé,' he explained. 'Say that Pepé sends his love and is of the best health, fighting for France.'

'We ought to be able to manage that,' asserted Ginger.

'Let's have a good look at the map,' suggested Algy. 'It would be as well to make ourselves absolutely *au fait** with the country.'

'I say, chaps, there's one thing we seem to have left out of the calculations,' put in Bertie. 'What about the jolly old princess?'

'What about her?' snorted Ginger. 'She was the cause of all the trouble. As far as I am concerned she can stay where she is, wherever that may be, or she can splash her own way out of the kettle of fish she put on to boil at Monte Carlo. Let's forget her.'

* French: acquainted.

Chapter 3
The Road to Monte Carlo

The following night, a little before twelve, Henri's Berline Briguet glided quietly at twenty thousand feet, on a southward course, over the grey limestone mass of the *departement** of France known as the Alpes Maritimes. The air was still, clear and warm, as it is at this pampered spot on three hundred days of the year. Far to the east the silver disc of the moon hung low over Italy, just clearing the peaks of the Ligurian Alps, which, like the edge of a saw, cut a jagged line across the sky. Into the west ran the deeply indented coastline of the French Riviera. To the south, glistening faintly to the moon, lay the age-old Mediterranean Sea, silent, deserted, centre of the bitterest wars of conquest since history began.

Henri nudged Algy, who sat beside him, and pointed ahead. '*Voila***!*' he breathed. 'Monaco.'

Algy could just make out a town of considerable size, standing, it seemed, knee-deep in the sea between two capes, one large, the other small and blunt, like a clenched fist.

Henri named them. 'On the left, Cap Martin. On the right, the little one, the rock of Monaco, where I live when I am home. Between, on the hill, Monte Carlo. The big white building, she is the casino. At the

* French equivalent of an English county
** French: There!

34

bottom of the hill on the right, the harbour, which we call La Condamine. Now we go down.'

Henri circled, losing height, for several minutes, paying close attention to the ground. At last he levelled out and held the machine steady.

'Now you go,' he said sharply. 'We glide straight up the valley. *Au revoir**.*'

'*Au revoir*, and many thanks,' answered Algy, and went aft to the cabin in which the others were waiting. 'This is it,' he announced crisply, and picked up a bulky bundle from the floor. Opening the door, he tossed it into space. 'See you on the carpet,' he said, and followed the bundle into the void.

As soon as the parachute opened he looked down, but it was still a little while before he could make out the details of the ground below. The terrain all looked much the same, the mountains dwarfed by his own altitude. But presently he saw that he was dropping into a long shallow valley, bounded on the eastward side by a slim road cut in the side of a mountain of considerable size, capped by an embattled citadel which he knew, from his study of the map, must be the fort on Mont Agel, overlooking the Principality of Monaco.

A minute later the ground rose sharply to meet him, and he braced himself for the shock of landing. He fell, but was soon on his feet, slipping out of his harness and rolling the parachute into a ball. He sat on it for a little while, listening, then whistled softly. The only other sound was the drone of the departing aircraft. An answering whistle came out of the moonlight; footsteps

* French: See you again

35

followed, and a minute or two later Bertie and Ginger appeared together.

Algy rose. 'Let's find the equipment,' he said quietly. 'Spread out and we shall cover more ground.'

It did not take them long to find the other parachute, which carried for its main load two strangely assorted articles—a guitar, and a sack of onions tied up in strings. Bertie picked up his guitar and Ginger sorted out the onions that were to lend colour to his role of a Spanish pedlar.

'Now we've got to find the broken-down house,' said Algy. 'I think I marked it on the road. Bring the stuff along.'

It was a steepish climb to the road, the road which Henri had told them, and confirmed on the map, ran from La Turbie, the mountain village behind Monaco, to Peille. They followed it for about half a mile, and then came upon the ruin they sought. It turned out to be a mere skeleton surrounded by loose stones that had once been the wall of a little garden. From near the gaping doorway sprang the customary twin cypress trees, one of which—so Bertie told them—is planted in the South of France to ensure Peace, and the other Prosperity.

The parachutes were thrown in a heap inside the building, and rocks from the broken walls piled over them until they were hidden from sight—a task that occupied them for the best part of an hour. No traffic of any sort passed along the road. Once a dog barked in the far distance, otherwise they might have been a thousand miles from civilization.

Algy straightened his back. 'That's that,' he remarked. 'From now we go our own ways, working on our own lines. The first most important thing to remember is that Henri will be at the Californie landing ground this day week, at twelve midnight, waiting for our signal that it is okay for him to land. It means that those who want to go home will have to be there on the dot. In the meantime, our temporary meeting-place, where we can compare notes, is on the Quai de Plaisance, in the Condamine, at the bottom of the steps that lead up to the water company's offices. Apparently there are steps all over the place in Monte Carlo. They call them *escaliers*. This particular lot goes by the name of the Escalier du Port. Is that all clear?'

'Yes,' answered Ginger.

'Absolutely,' confirmed Bertie.

'Right, then off we go. You can go first, Ginger. Bertie will give you ten minutes and then follow. I'll go last. Keep straight on down the road for a mile and a narrow cutting on the right will take you down to La Turbie, which sits astride the Grande Corniche Road. Cross the road and you'll see the old rack-and-pinion railway line that drops down into Monaco. Actually it comes out in Monte Carlo, on a bit of an elevation overlooking the casino gardens. Everyone has got plenty of money, so there should be no difficulty about food.'

Ginger pulled down over his right ear the rather greasy black beret that he wore, and shouldered his onions. 'So long,' he said, and set off down the road.

He knew just where he was, for he had studied the map of Monaco and its environs until he had a clear mental picture of the district in his mind. He had also read a recommended guide-book, which he had found more interesting than he expected. He knew just what he was going to do, for the choice of possibilities was narrow and he had had ample time to formulate a plan of action. Obviously, the first thing was to ascertain if Biggles had left any written messages at either of the places he had named, the Quai de Plaisance at Monte Carlo, and Jock's Bar below the promenade at Nice. The others would probably do the same, but that didn't matter. He would go to Monte Carlo first, because that was the nearer. He plodded on, whistling softly, feeling curiously like the part he had decided to play. The road was deserted, as he expected it would be at such an hour. Not a light showed anywhere.

Twenty minutes' sharp walk and a cutting dipped suddenly to the right, past some cottages. An incline of perhaps a quarter of a mile brought him to a main road, which he had learned from his guide-book was the Grande Corniche, the famous Aurelian Way of the Roman conquerors of Britain. The old Roman posting village of La Turbie lay before him. If confirmation were needed, it was supplied by the towering marble monument erected nearly two thousand years before to the Emperor Augustus. He was amazed at its size. With a strange sensation of living in the past he walked a little way along the road until he came to another time-worn landmark, the Roman milestone number 604—the 604th mile from Rome. And there, almost at his feet, began the overgrown rails of the disused railway, dropping almost sheer into Monte Carlo. Moving his position slightly, he could see the famous international holiday resort snuggling in its little bay, nearly two thousand feet below. On the left of it, Cap Martin thrust a black claw into the sea. On the right, the castle making it unmistakable, was the blunt headland of Monaco itself. Silhouetted against the sky, a short distance from where he stood, rose a single stone column, which he again knew from his book was all that remained of the formidable gallows on which innumerable corsairs, in the distant past, had ended their careers of pillage. Beyond, rolling away, it seemed, to infinity, was the Mediterranean, as devoid of movement as a sheet of black glass. That same sea, he reflected, from the very viewpoint on which he now stood, must have been the last earthly scene on which the condemned pirates had looked.

He was about to start the descent when footsteps approaching from the village sent him creeping into the ink-black shadow of a broad-leafed fig tree. He lay flat and remained motionless. The footsteps came nearer.

A voice said, 'But I tell you I did hear something.'

Another voice answered, 'It must have been a dog or a cat.'

The first voice replied, 'It sounded to me more like someone walking.'

Raising his eyes, Ginger saw two peaked uniform caps outlined against the sky.

'Anybody there?' called one of the men, sharply, speaking, of course, in French.

Ginger held his breath.

There was a short interval of silence; then the two men, talking in low tones, strolled away in the direction from which they had come.

As far as Ginger was concerned it was a disconcerting incident, for it warned him that, dead though the country seemed, police or soldiers—he knew not which—were on patrol. Was this just routine, he wondered, or were they on the watch for somebody, and if so, who? This was a question which no amount of surmise could answer, so after waiting for a little while he began a cautious descent of the railway, stopping from time to time to listen, for the unexpected appearance of the two men had tightened his nerves.

He had no intention of going straight down into the town, for the fact of his being abroad at such an hour could hardly fail to arouse the suspicions of the Italian secret police who, the Air Commodore had said, were numerous in Monaco. If that were so, they would certainly take notice of strangers, probably more so by night than by day. So when he was within easy distance of the abandoned railway station he left the track, and finding a comfortable cranny in the herb-covered hillside, he lay down to wait for daylight. In any case there was nothing he could do in the dark. The air was soft and warm, so with the perfume of wild lavender in his nostrils he settled down to sleep.

When he awoke, with a start, the sun was a ball of fire balanced on the horizon beyond Cap Martin, its rays pouring gold across tiny dancing waves. Sounds of life arose from the town, so after a cautious survey of his immediate surroundings, he picked up the onions and continued his descent.

There was no one in the ramshackle station buildings, but on leaving them he nearly collided with a man in a white, red-braided uniform, who was standing at the top of the steps outside, swinging a white *batôn**
from a leathern loop. Ginger knew that he was a policeman of some sort, probably a Monégasque.

'Hello! Where have you come from?' asked the man.

Ginger answered in his best French. 'A fellow must sleep. Why pay for a room when the weather is fine?'

The policeman smiled and looked at the onions. 'Spanish?'

* French: Short stick carried by the police similar to a truncheon

40

'*Si.*'

'I could do with an onion to take home,' suggested the *gendarme**. 'I'm just going off duty.'

'If I had given an onion to every *gendarme* who has asked for one since I left Barcelona, I should have none to sell,' answered Ginger, not a little relieved that his companion was such an amiable fellow.

'Just one?'

'You find the bread and I'll supply the onions,' suggested Ginger smiling.

'Bread? *Oh la la*. It isn't bread any longer. Still, I suppose it's better than nothing. Let's see what we can do. Descend, my friend.'

They walked together down the steps to a café where, under a faded awning bearing the name, Café de Lyons, a man in shirt sleeves was wiping down small round tables. A conversation ensued, following which the café proprietor, grinning, went inside and returned with half a loaf of dark-coloured bread and a carafe of thin red wine.

The *gendarme* unbuttoned his tunic. 'We can still eat and drink,' he said. 'Untie your onions my young friend.'

Ginger set an onion in front of each of them, and the meal began.

'How are things in Spain?' asked the *gendarme*.

'In Barcelona, where I come from, bad,' returned Ginger.

'Not worse than here, I should say,' observed the proprietor sadly, as he sliced his onion. 'You know,' he went on, 'I have often bought Spanish onions, but I never saw any like these.'

* French: policeman

Ginger hadn't thought of that, but he kept his head. 'We are trying new sorts,' he said airily. 'They say the government is importing seeds from America.'

'I can't say I think much of these; they are too strong,' asserted the *gendarme*, with tears running down his cheeks. '*Mon Dieu*!* They are as bad as English onions. I ate one once, when I went to visit my sister in London.'

Ginger grinned. 'What do you expect? How can they grow onions in England, where the rain never stops?'

'No, that's true, poor devils,' agreed the proprietor. He glanced around. 'Talking about the English, they say there was an Englishman here the other day—a spy.'

'Who says?' asked Ginger, grimacing as he sipped the rough wine.

'Everyone knows about it,' answered the proprietor, and would have gone on, but the *gendarme* stopped him with a frown.

'It is better not to talk of these things,' said he.

The proprietor sighed, which gave Ginger an idea of what he thought of the state of things.

Ginger passed off an awkward situation by offering to sell him some onions.

'They're too strong,' said the proprietor, shaking his head.

'They go all the farther for that in the pot,' declared Ginger.

'That's the truth, by God,' said the *gendarme*, wiping his eyes. 'I should say this onion I am eating would stop a tank.'

'Now food is scarce, the idea is to make things go a long way,' argued Ginger.

* French: My God!

42

'How much?' asked the proprietor.

'Ten francs the kilo.'

'Too much. I'll give you five.'

'Nine.'

'Six.'

'I'll take eight, and not a *sou* less,' swore Ginger.

'Six.'

'Seven if you take two kilos and throw in a sardine to eat with the bread.'

'*C'est-ca*.*' The proprietor fetched the scales, and the sardines. Between them they weighed off the two kilogrammes.

'One for luck,' said the proprietor, helping himself to two onions and throwing them in the scales.

'*Carramba**!*' growled Ginger. 'And you call us Spaniards thieves.'

Shouting with laughter the cheerful *gendarme* got up. 'I have a wife who expects me to come home,' he said, putting an onion in his pocket. '*Au revoir.*'

Ginger was in no hurry. His introduction to the café proprietor offered possibilities of obtaining information, and he prepared to explore them.

'What's all this talk about a spy?' he asked casually.

The proprietor shrugged his shoulders. 'What a question! There are more spies in this place than there were sharpers before the war.'

'You said something about an Englishman?' prompted Ginger, without looking up.

The Monégasque leaned forward. 'Nobody knows the truth about that,' he asserted. 'But they say there

* French: that's it, OK
** Spanish exclamation similar to Blimey! or My God!

43

was a woman in the affair, and between them they killed five Italian police.'

'Phew! Were they caught?'

'Some say they were, others say they were not. Some say they were both shot. Others say they are still hiding in Monaco, which accounts for the Italian police everywhere. But there, nobody knows what to believe in times like these.'

'That's true,' agreed Ginger.

The proprietor bent still nearer, breathing a pungent mixture of garlic and onions into Ginger's face. 'They say Zabani is mixed up in this, and that he has been put on the spot by the Camorra* for double-crossing one of them.'

'Camorra? I thought Mussolini boasted that he had wiped out all the Italian secret societies?'

The proprietor winked. 'Franco bragged that he had wiped out your Spanish society, the Black Hand,' he countered. 'Has he?'

'For my part,' said Ginger slowly, 'I should doubt it.'

The Monégasque eyed him narrowly. 'You're not one of them I hope?'

'Me?' Ginger laughed. 'Not likely. I don't want a knife in my back.'

'Nor me. Once the Camorra sets its mark on a man he's as good as dead. If Zabani has betrayed one of them, God help him—not that he deserves any help.'

'He's a bad one, eh?'

'If half what they say of him is true, he is a match for Satan himself.'

'Is he Italian?'

---

* A secret criminal society, similar to the mafia

'Yes.'

'If he is an Italian why does he live here?'

'Like others, to gamble in the casino. He is always in the gaming rooms. He is not Monégasque, you understand. The Monégasques do not go near the tables. I am a Monégasque.' The man spoke proudly.

The statement reminded Ginger that he had meant to ask Henri just what was a Monégasque. He realized of course that the word described the real natives of Monaco, but from what race they originally sprang he did not know. It seemed to be an opportunity to find out.

'What is a Monégasque that you are so proud of being one?' he enquired.

'*Zut!* The question!'

'I am a stranger here,' reminded Ginger.

'A Monégasque, my young friend, is—a Monégasque.'

'Not French?'

'Name of a name! No.'

'Italian perhaps?'

'No, although there are many Italians here, good Italians, who obey the laws of Monaco. Some came to avoid the conscription in Italy—and who shall blame them? There are few true Monégasques—three thousand perhaps. They rule themselves. Most of them live on the Rock.'

'Where did they come from in the first place?'

'Ah! That is another question. First of all, long long ago, lived here the Ligurians, wild people with stone clubs. Then came the Phœnicians—they built many of the old villages round about. Later came the Greeks. Then came the Romans who, to mark their conquest, built the great monument at La Turbie—look, you can see it from here. After that came all sorts of people—

45

French, Italians, Lombards, adventurers from the sea, yes, even English, the Crusaders, and such people, as well as Christian prisoners brought by the Saracens. Between them all they leave a type which long ago became called the Monégasque. Do not, my young friend, confuse us with the French, or the Italians, although because we are so near to France and Italy most of us speak the languages of those countries.'

'I see,' said Ginger.

'But I can't sit here talking,' went on the proprietor, rising. 'It is too early in the morning. I have work to do. Call next time you are passing and I may buy some more onions—but next time bring the Spanish. *Au revoir.*'

'*Au revoir, monsieur.*'

Perceiving that there was nothing more to be learned, and well satisfied with the smattering of news he had picked up, Ginger slung his lightened burden over his shoulder and departed. He still did not know what had happened to Biggles, but the bare fact that even in Monaco there was a doubt about his fate, was encouraging. It had evidently leaked out that the princess's betrayer, Zabani, was concerned with the affair. The café proprietor's reference to the Camorra, the dreaded Italian secret society, in connection with Zabani, was a new and interesting piece of information.

Thus pondered Ginger as he strode on towards the sea, which could be observed beyond the casino gardens. People were beginning to move about in the streets, ordinary people, as far as he could judge, mostly fellows in simple working clothes, or blue overalls. Their faces were brown, and while a few walked as if with a definite object in view, the majority slouched about, listless, without any set purpose, creating an atmosphere very different from the mental picture he

46

had always held of the famous society playground. Police were conspicuous, although for the most part they seemed to be content to stand at street corners and gossip. They were easily identified by their uniforms. There were the local police, the Monégasques, in the service of the Prince of Monaco. They wore white drill suits with scarlet facings—the colours of the principality—and sun helmets. It was one of these who had invited Ginger to the Café de Lyons. There were a few French *gendarmes*, in dark blue tunics and khaki slacks; they were usually in pairs. There were also Italians who, officially or unofficially—Ginger was not sure which—were evidently in occupation. There were a few cars outside the big hotels which, like the gardens, and everything else, had a look of neglect. Outside the imposing Hotel de Paris there was a saloon car carrying a swastika pennant on the radiator cap, and another flaunting the Italian flag. He passed without stopping, and going over to the ornamental balustrade on the far side of the road, saw the little port of Monaco below him.

It was the neatest, tidiest port he had ever seen, largely artificial, having been formed by the construction of two moles, one springing from the Monaco village side, and the other from Monte Carlo. Between the ends of the moles, a gap gave access to the open sea. Within the small square harbour itself there were no ships of any size—a few yachts at moorings on one side, and a collection of small craft on the other.

As Ginger looked down, the broad walk on the near side was, he knew, the Quai de Plaisance, his immediate objective. On the opposite side of the harbour, known as the Quai de Commerce, some men were rolling barrels. A short walk took him to the offices of the water company, beside which a steep flight of steps, named the Escalier du Port, led down to the Quai de Plaisance.

Descending to the quay he found himself on a broad concrete pavement, bounded on one side by a high stone wall, and on the other, by deep water. He looked about him. The only people in sight were a few elderly men, and children, fishing with simple bamboo poles. A short distance to the right a man was mopping out a slim motor-boat that floated lightly on its own inverted image. After a cursory glance the people fishing paid no attention to him, so he began to stroll along the wall looking for writing in blue pencil. He did not really expect to find any, but the bare possibility, now that he was actually on the spot, gave him a curious thrill.

He walked along towards the outer mole, his hopes dwindling as he approached the end without seeing anything resembling what he sought. The only writing was the usual French warning notice against the sticking of bills. Returning, he was about to examine the wall beyond the foot of the steps by which he had descended to the quay, when an incident occurred which at first astonished, and then alarmed him.

Along the inner side of the harbour, which ran at right angles to, and connected the Quai de Plaisance with the Quai de Commerce, there was a broad stone pavement similar to the one on which he walked. This pavement was obviously the part given over to local fishermen. It was backed by a number of tiny houses, and boat sheds, from which shipways ran down into the water. There was quite a collection of small craft, both in and out of the water. A number of fishermen, dressed in the usual sun-bleached blue trousers and shirts, were gossiping as they worked on their boats or mended their nets.

From this direction now appeared Bertie, made conspicuous by his guitar. He was strolling along unconcernedly, apparently on his way to examine the wall of the Quai de Plaisance. Watching, Ginger saw him—for no apparent reason—stop suddenly, back a few paces, turn, and walk quickly away. A moment later, the boatman who had been mopping out the motorboat, sprang up on to the quay and hurried after him. Ginger was not sure, but he thought he heard the boatman call out. Bertie glanced back over his shoulder, and seeing that he was pursued, quickened his pace. The boatman broke into a run.

In a disinterested way Ginger had already noticed this man, first on account of the innumerable patches on his overalls, and secondly, because of his outstanding ugliness. His face might have been that of a heathen idol, carved out of dark wood. To make matters worse his nose was bent, and his eyes, due to a pronounced cast in one of them, appeared to look in different directions. The effect of this was to make it impossible to tell in precisely what direction the man was looking, a state of affairs which Ginger, conscious of the secret nature of his task, found disconcerting.

Still followed by the boatman Bertie disappeared behind a colourful array of sails that were hanging up to dry.

Ginger watched all this with serious misgivings. It was obvious that the boatman was trying to overtake Bertie, and he wondered why. He watched for some time, and the fact that neither of them returned did nothing to allay his anxiety. When twenty minutes had passed, and still Bertie did not return, Ginger gave it up, and continued his interrupted survey of the wall.

Chapter 4
The Writing on the Wall

A dozen paces Ginger took and then stopped short, his heart palpitating, Bertie's strange behaviour forgotten. For there, before his eyes—indeed, within a foot of his face after he had taken a swift step forward—was what he sought, what he prayed might be there, yet dare not truly hope to find. It was writing on the wall, bold blue lettering on the pale grey limestone; and the first thing that caught his excited attention was the final symbol of the message. It was a triangle, quite small, but clear and unmistakable. The actual message consisted of three words only. They were: CHEZ ROSSI. PERNOD.

Ginger's first reaction as his eyes drank in the cryptic communication was one of disappointment. Doubtless the message contained vital information, but at the moment it told him nothing. Worse still, there was no indication of when it had been written. That Biggles had written the words he had no doubt whatever, and that they were intended to convey important news was equally certain. But—here was the rub—had the message been written before the catastrophe at the Californie landing ground, or afterwards? Upon that factor everything depended. Whatever the words might mean, reflected Ginger, they did not tell him what he was most anxious to know. Was Biggles alive or dead?

He did not stand staring at the message. There was no need for that. The words were engraved on his memory. Nobody appeared to be watching him, so he strolled over and sat down on one of the many benches provided for visitors in less troublous times. It was easy enough to see why the message had been expressed as a meaningless phrase. Obviously, Biggles could not write in plain English. In fact, it seemed that English words had been deliberately avoided. He pondered on the puzzle.

Chez Rossi was almost certainly the name of an establishment, probably a café, bar or restaurant. The word *chez*, meaning 'the house of,' or 'the home of,' was a common prefix to public places of that sort. Rossi was probably the name of the owner. Chez Rossi, therefore, was most likely the name of a bar or restaurant in Monaco, run by a man named Rossi. At any rate, the original proprietor would have been thus named. Pernod was a word he did not know, although it sounded like another name. That was something which could perhaps be discovered at the café, bar, or whatever the establishment turned out to be. Clearly, the thing to do was to find out if there was such a place, and if there was, pay it a visit.

Remembering Bertie and his peculiar behaviour he looked along the back of the harbour where he had last seen him, and even walked a short distance in that direction; but there was no sign of him, nor of the boatman with the mahogany face who had followed him. He waited for a little while, and then, loath to waste any more time, made his way up into Monte Carlo, his intention being to call on the friendly proprietor of the Café de Lyons to inquire about the Chez Rossi. He would know if there was such a place.

For the sake of appearance he called at several shops

and houses *en route**, and did, in fact, dispose of so much of his stock that he became afraid he might sell out, which did not suit him. So with the two strings that remained he strode on to the Café de Lyons.

It now presented a different appearance. Many of the chairs, which in accordance with French custom had been put out on the pavement, were occupied by people reading newspapers, with a glass or a cup at their elbows. However, this made little difference to Ginger, who had no intention of staying. He managed to catch the eye of the proprietor who, recognizing him, and evidently noticing that his onions had diminished, congratulated him on his sales ability. With that he would have gone on with his work, but Ginger caught him by the arm.

'One moment, *monsieur*,' he appealed. 'I am told that I might find a customer at Chez Rossi. Could you direct me?'

'But certainly,' was the willing response. 'It is at the back of the town. Take the Boulevard St. Michel, here on the right, and the second turning again on the right. At the corner of the first *escalier* you will see the Rossi bar-restaurant.'

'*Merci, monsieur*,' thanked Ginger, and turned away to the boulevard which, before the war, had clearly been fashionable shops and hotels. But when he took the second turning on the right, the scene and atmosphere changed even more suddenly than a visitor to London finds when turning out of Oxford Street into Soho. This, obviously, was where the people lived, the working classes, the permanent residents, as opposed to the wealthy visitors. The street was narrow. Tall but

* French: on the way

52

shabby whitewashed houses rose high on either side. Laundry, strings of bright-hued garments, stretched from window to window. A drowsy hum hung on air that was heavy with sunshine. Caged birds twittered. Through narrow open doorways he saw families eating, lounging or sleeping. Music crept from tiny cafés. Occasionally he passed an unfenced garden overgrown with cacti, geraniums and trailing vines, or shops where objects for which no earthly use could be discovered mixed up with nails, dried fish, bundles of dried herbs, oil and vinegar. Sometimes an *escalier*, a crazy flight of steps without number, wound into mysterious distances.

Ten minutes walk brought him within sight of his objective, made conspicuous by a faded red awning bearing in white letters the name of the establishment— Chez Rossi. A smaller notice announced the place to be a bar-restaurant. So far so good, thought Ginger. Closer inspection revealed it to be one of the small restaurants, with a bar on one side, common in all French towns. Judging by the name, mused Ginger, the proprietor was, or the original proprietor had been, an Italian. If the latter, the name of the business would not be changed.

Ginger pushed aside the curtain that hung over the entrance and saw at a glance that the place was a typical Mediterranean eating house—small, with numerous tables set uncomfortably close together, but clean. The customary smell, an evasive aroma of garlic, fish and herbs, peculiar to British nostrils, hung in the air.

There were perhaps half a dozen people present, all men, small, dark Italians, southern French or Monégasques. At any rate, they were all typical

Mediterraneos. All were eating the same dish which, by the pungent smell, was fish soup, highly flavoured. This was being served by a swarthy, black-browed, heavily-moustached, shirt-sleeved waiter, a middle-aged man with dark, suspicious eyes, and a smooth deportment that enabled him to move among the tables without colliding with them.

Ginger crossed to an unoccupied table, dropped his onions on the floor, and sat down.

The waiter approached. 'Soup, *monsieur?*'

'What is there to eat?' asked Ginger, thinking that as it was now noon he might as well take the opportunity of having a good meal.

'Fish soup, *monsieur*, ten francs, with bread and wine included. We serve only one dish.'

Ginger nodded assent. As the waiter went through to the kitchen to fetch the food he wondered if by any chance he was the proprietor, Rossi, or the Pernod referred to in the writing on the wall. But this possibility was quickly dispelled when one of the other customers called him by name. The name was Mario.

Who, then, was Pernod? wondered Ginger. The curious thing about the word was, every now and then it touched a chord in his memory, as though he had heard it, or seen it, before; but he could not quite remember where; once or twice he nearly had it, but in the end it eluded him and he gave up the mental quest. Instead, having nothing else to do, he started to make a closer scrutiny of his surroundings. It ended abruptly, with a shock. He stared, doubting for once the evidence of his eyes. For there, confronting him across the room, was a single word in bold letters. The word was PERNOD. It was printed on a card, below a picture of a bottle.

Evidently an advertisement for a beverage, the card hung on the wall, suspended from a nail.

The effect of this unexpected revelation was so startling that it took Ginger a minute to recover his composure. He remembered now where he had seen the word. He had, in fact, seen it scores of times, for Pernod was one of the most popular drinks in France, and the most widely advertised; and on that account there was nothing remarkable about its presence in the restaurant. Was it coincidence? wondered Ginger. No, he decided, the card, in some way, was linked up through the writing on the wall, with Biggles. A quick glance round the room satisfied him that the other customers were concerned only with their own affairs, so he crossed over, and with hands that trembled slightly unhooked the card from the wall. Holding it low, he returned to his place at the table. He examined the front of the card. There was nothing on it that had not been printed. He turned it over, and his heart gave a bound when his eyes fell on a line of blue writing, ending in a triangle. This is what he read:

Villa V—Heil Hitler. Mario is a waiter, *par excellence**.

Ginger stared at the words. Then, with a start he looked up to see Mario, evidently the waiter *par excellence* referred to in the message, regarding him with attentive, suspicious eyes. In his hand he held a plate of soup, which, seeing that he had been observed, he put on the table with a show of professional pride. Ginger said nothing. He could think of nothing to say, or do, except, when the waiter retired, rehang the showcard in its position on the wall.

Mario returned to put bread and wine on the table.

* French: of the highest standard

At brief intervals his dark eyes met those of his customer. They gleamed with suspicion, and once Ginger thought he detected a queer expression of questioning alarm, as though the waiter expected him to say something, yet was afraid. He felt, too, that he ought to say something, give an explanation of his strange behaviour, but he still did not know what he could say without leading up to the real object of his visit, and that, he decided, was premature.

The waiter retired and he settled down to his soup, which he found was of excellent flavour and satisfying. While he ate he pondered on the curious development of his problem. As in the case of the Quai de Plaisance, there was no indication of when the message had been written. Where did Mario fit into the scheme? He was, the message asserted, an excellent waiter. What did it matter what sort of waiter he was, good or bad? The word waiter had been underlined. Did that imply the second meaning of the word—that Mario was waiting for something, or somebody; if so, for whom or what was he waiting? There were two ways of finding out. One was to ask him, a procedure which, Ginger felt, was hardly likely to be successful. The other way was to watch him.

The first part of the message was easier to understand. Villa V was obviously the Villa Valdora to which the princess had flown for sanctuary, the house of the Italian who had betrayed her. Its name, coupled with the words Heil Hitler, was a clear indication that Zabani was an enemy. But what concern was that of Mario?

Ginger lingered for a little while, thinking the matter over, and not quite sure what to do next. In the end he decided first to try watching Mario, and if that led to nothing—well, he would take the bull by the horns and try the more direct method of questioning him. He paid his bill and went out. But he did not go far. He turned, and strolling back along the pavement, glanced in passing through the open door. Quick though he had been to return, Mario—or someone—had been faster. The Pernod show-card had gone. That proved, if proof were needed, that Mario was in some way mixed up with the affair; but just where he fitted in was not easy to see.

Deep in thought, Ginger strolled back down the narrow street. He noticed that most people were taking the usual after-lunch siesta, and he thought he might as well do the same, so he descended to the Condamine and sat on the same seat that he had used earlier in the day. This would enable him to rest and at the same time keep watch for Algy or Bertie. He was anxious to talk over with them the result of his investigations; perhaps they would be able to unravel the mystery.

Neither put in an appearance. All the afternoon he waited, and still they did not come, which struck him as odd. He could not imagine what they were doing. He gave them another hour, and when they still did not appear he walked back up to Monte Carlo, offering his onions for sale whenever policemen were near at hand. For a little while he toyed with the idea of going to Nice to see if there was any writing on the wall of Jock's Bar. But he saw that he could not do that and at the same time keep watch on Mario. Nice was a fair distance away. Jock's Bar would have to wait. He could go there when he had finished with the Chez Rossi.

Slowly he made his way to the street in which the restaurant was situated, and taking up a position from which he could watch both the front and the side door, prepared to wait. It was now six o'clock, and the sun was sinking behind the towering headland called the *Tête de Chien*. The sky turned pink, then mauve. Presently night took possession. Ginger drew nearer. From time to time a customer entered or left the restaurant. Once he looked in through a window and saw an elderly slattern of a woman serving. It was a slow, weary vigil, and he was again considering the idea of approaching Mario direct when he saw him come out of the side door.

Ginger shrank back into deep shadow and watched. The waiter was now dressed in quite a smart suit of some dark material. He looked up and down the street. His manner was brisk, alert, like that of a cat which, after drowsing all day, comes to life when darkness falls. Another glance up and down the street, and then, as though bound on a definite errand, the waiter set off at a sharp walk in the direction opposite the one from which Ginger had approached.

This was better, thought Ginger, as he followed.

Mario walked so fast that he found it no easy matter to keep him in sight—at any rate, until he dropped down a narrow *escalier* which emerged in a more fashionable part of the town. The street being wider, visibility improved.

From this street Mario turned into an avenue, the name of which Ginger did not know, but which was more in accord with his mental picture of Monte Carlo. Signs of wealth and luxury were everywhere. On both sides of the road, behind marble balustrades and wrought-iron gates, stood splendid villas, tall, white, stately, built in the Italian style, each standing in its own garden of exotic shrubs and palms. Oleander trees, pink-flowered, with oranges and lemons heavy with fruit, lined the drives. The climbing magenta bougain-villea hung in great masses from balconies and per-golas.

Near the end of this avenue Ginger discovered, to his dismay, that he had lost his man. He seemed to disappear into the night. Walking quickly to the place where he had last seen him, he found a pillared entrance drive at the end of which stood a villa more like a small palace than a house. A name on each pillar stood out in black letters on a white background. And as Ginger read the name he understood. It was the Villa Valdora.

A quick glance up and down the deserted avenue and Ginger was in the drive, nerves tingling, advancing warily towards the house. Not a light showed any-where, but that, he saw, was because every window was heavily curtained. Between tall windows, at the near end of the house, was the main entrance, a noble portal approached by a broad flight of marble steps.

Ginger was at a loss to know what to do. He did not forget that Zabani was an enemy. Obviously, he could not go boldly to the front door—nor any other door, for that matter. He was in no doubt at all that it was into this house that Mario had vanished, so, with ears and eyes alert, he backed into some dark-leaved shrubs to watch events, or for some sign that might indicate in what part of the house Mario had gone. By watching the drive he would at least see him emerge.

He had not long to wait, and then the waiter's exit was made in a manner entirely unexpected. A window at the side of the villa, on the ground floor, was quietly opened. A rustle, and a figure showed black against the white wall. Without a sound it dropped to the ground and began moving with feline stealth towards the drive. It passed within a yard of where Ginger was crouching, and for a moment he distinctly saw the face. It was Mario—but not the suave waiter of the Chez Rossi. His eyes were staring; his lips were parted, and he was panting like a man who has just run a gruelling race. Suddenly he darted down the drive and disappeared in the direction from which he had come. Ginger could tell by the footsteps that he was running, and by the time he had recovered from his surprise he knew that it was too late to follow.

For a few seconds he was the prey of hesitation. Should he return to the restaurant—or what? What had happened in the villa? Perhaps this would presently be divulged. But when a minute or two had passed and nothing happened, he dumped his onions under a shrub and went over to the open window. He thought he might hear something, or see something. But the place was in darkness. The whole house was as quiet as a tomb. Who had Mario come to see? Was the princess somewhere in this sinister building, after all? And Biggles?

Encouraged by the silence, Ginger took the window-sill in his hands and vaulted up. Another movement and he was inside. A flash of his torch revealed a wide corridor. At one end a door stood ajar. A dozen paces took him to it. Not a sound came from inside. With his heart thumping against his ribs, he pushed the door wide open. Darkness. Nothing happened. He entered.

Advancing slowly, the light of his torch played on such rare and costly furnishings that he held his breath in sheer amazement. Magnificent paintings hung on the walls. In cabinets, and on pieces of furniture, glass and china gleamed. It might have been the interior of an oriental palace. Having explored the walls, the beam of light dropped lower. It fell on a cabinet of exquisite workmanship, and passed on to a massive carved desk. And there it stopped, stopped while Ginger's heart missed a beat, and then tore on at a gallop. He knew now why Mario had been to the Villa Valdora.

Across the desk was slumped, face downwards, the body of a man, a plump man in a black suit. That, for a moment, was all that Ginger could see. And it was enough. For several seconds he stood rooted to the ground by sheer horror. Something was dripping, dripping horribly. Bracing himself, he took a nervous pace nearer, and saw something else. From between the man's shoulder blades projected the haft of a knife. Surrounding the haft was a disc of white paper.

Trembling, breathless from shock, Ginger went still nearer, his eyes on the paper. On it had been scrawled, large, so that it almost encircled the handle of the knife, the single letter C. That was all. There was nothing more, except that he noted that the dead man had evidently tried to use the telephone, for he had lifted the receiver and still clutched it in his hand.

With the passing of the first shock recollection came to Ginger of where he was and what he was doing. He had seen enough—indeed, he had seen a good deal more than he had bargained for. It was time to get out. War was one thing, but he had no desire to be mixed up with murder.

He was on his way to the door when he heard a car skid to a standstill. It was followed by a babble of excited voices. A bell pealed with an incredible amount of noise. Fists thumped on the front door.

These sounds nearly threw Ginger into a panic. Running to the nearest window, he half drew the curtain and looked out. He saw what he expected. Outside clustered a group of *gendarmes*.

Ginger made for the window through which he had entered. There was no one outside it, but as he jumped to the ground a man came round the end of the house. There was a shout. Ginger bolted. He fled down the drive, past the people who were at the front door, and reached the avenue. Shouts, quickly followed by pistol shots, followed him. A whistle shrilled. He tore on. He had no idea where he was going, nor did he much care; his entire faculties were concentrated on getting as far as possible from the Villa Valdora in the shortest possible time. As he ran he looked desperately for a side turning, but for some time there was none. Shots were still being fired and he could hear bullets whistling unpleasantly close. At last, to his infinite relief, he came to an *escalier* leading downwards. He turned into it, and at that very moment a bullet hit him in the thigh. It was as though someone had struck him with a mallet.

The blow brought him down, but he was up again in an instant. There was no pain, but as he sped on down the steps he could feel blood squelching in his shoe. A deadly weakness seized him at the knees, but he kept going. The steps seemed interminable, and when he reached the bottom his faintness was such that he had to cling to some railings to steady himself. A moment's pause and then, like a hunted fox, he ran on. All the time there had been sounds of pursuit behind him, but he knew that the car in which the police had arrived would be unable to follow him down the *escalier*.

He ran blindly, fighting nausea. He felt no pain, only a ghastly sickness. He crossed a road and found himself in what appeared to be a sort of market-place. Happening to glance behind, he saw with horror that he was leaving a trail of blood, a trail that a child could have followed. Gasping, he looked wildly about him for a place to hide. In a garden close by, a line of washing hung like flags at a fête. He entered and tore down a linen shirt. Sitting on a seat, with the rag he made a pad and bandage for his wound, anything to stop the flow of blood that was sapping his strength and marking his course. While he was doing it several men passed at a run. Occasionally a whistle was blown.

Still feeling sick, but relieved that he had stopped the bleeding, he took the only way that seemed to lead from the hue and cry. This was a ramp, a long incline that led up to the rock on which the ancient village of Monaco was built. Sometimes the path broke into steps. He thought it would never end. Below him to the left, in the light of the stars, he could see the harbour and the Quai de Plaisance. He knew that he was getting near the end of his endurance, and was afraid that he might faint. His head began to swim, and he found it necessary to pull himself up by the railings. Struggling on with the desperation of sheer determination to get to the top, he passed under a stone arch and found himself on a wide gravel space. On the far side the palace loomed enormous against the dark blue sky. About him were statues, old cannon, and neatly piled heaps of cannon-balls. On the left, occasional paved alleys, too narrow to be called streets, wound into the heart of the old town.

Like a wounded rabbit making for its burrow, he went to the nearest, and happening to glance up, saw a name that struck sharply on his memory. It was Rue Marinière. In such a turmoil was his brain that for a moment he could not recall where he had heard the name before. Then he remembered. It was the street in which lived the mother of their Monégasque pilot, Henri Ducoste. Number six, Henri had said. They had offered, if it were possible, to deliver a message, but when the offer had been made Ginger little imagined how it would be delivered.

Seeking number six, he staggered along the narrow street, with his torch, looking at the numbers on the doors. It was darker than it had been—or was it? Ginger wasn't sure. He wasn't sure of anything except that the walls seemed to recede and then rush in upon him in a frightening manner. Doors danced before his eyes. He saw number six, as through a mist. In his attempt to knock he fell against the door. He clutched the handle. The door flew open with a crash. There was a startled cry inside and a girl appeared, lamp in hand, peering forward in an attitude of alarm.

The picture was engraved indelibly on Ginger's brain. All he could see was the girl, a girl of about eighteen years of age, who from the sombre manner of her dress was a Monégasque. Her complexion was pale, the indefinable tint of sun-warmed ivory, and her skin was without blemish. Her features, untouched by cosmetics, were perfect. Her lips were slightly parted, revealing small teeth of startling whiteness. The carriage of her head, on shapely shoulders, was proud, although her dark eyes were wide with fear. Her hair was jet black, parted flat in the middle, half concealing two tiny gold rings that depended from her ears.

For a moment Ginger stared at her, his brain reeling. Then, as the picture began to fade, he staggered forward.

'Pepé,' he gasped. Then again, 'Pepé.' He tried to say more, but the words would not come. Only his lips moved, noiselessly, while the light of the lamp seemed to fail. Darkness rushed in upon him. He felt himself falling—falling—falling . . .

Chapter 5
Bertie Meets a Friend

Ginger had not been mistaken when he saw Bertie at the harbour. After he had left Algy and Bertie on the Peille road they had tossed up to decide who should go to Jock's Bar, at Nice, and who to Monte Carlo. Algy had won, and for reasons which he did not divulge had chosen Nice. Bertie, therefore, had walked along to La Turbie, where he had decided to start his investigations. Knowing the district intimately he perceived that if, as had been stated, Biggles had fled from Monaco to Nice by way of the 'top' Corniche road, he must have passed through La Turbie. The people there might know something about it, and what they knew would certainly be known at the hotel. There was nothing he could do at two o'clock in the morning, so he curled up in an olive grove, slept until dawn, and then, singing to himself, made his way to the hotel which stands almost opposite the disused railway. An old man and a young girl were already astir, and they wished him a cheerful *bon jour**.

Over breakfast of a roll and some poor coffee he proceeded cautiously with his inquiries, but without success. Either the people knew nothing, or they were not prepared to talk. Conversation ended abruptly when four *gendarmes* who had evidently been on night duty came in and ordered coffee. Under the pretence

* French: Good day

66

of tuning his guitar Bertie listened to their conversation for a little while, but they seemed more concerned with the battle of Egypt, which was then proceeding, than local affairs; so, deciding that he had wasted enough time, he slung the instrument across his back and took the road to Monte Carlo. He was quite prepared to be stopped and questioned; and he was, twice, in each case by an Italian policeman and a French *gendarme*, who appeared to work in couples. His answers satisfied them and he was allowed to pass.

Arriving in Monte Carlo he walked down the hill to the Condamine, and from there turned into the Quai de Plaisance. He saw that Ginger was already there, so he decided to join him and ask him how he was progressing. But before he could do so he was startled to hear himself hailed by name. Looking in the direction from which the voice had come he saw a man in well-patched overalls standing in a motor-boat, an incredibly ugly man with a cast in one eye. He recognised him at once, for he had known him for years. The man was, in fact, a mechanic named François Budette, a Monégasque who before the war he had employed to service his motor-boat during the races. The boat in which the man was standing, named *Bluebird*, was his own. He had abandoned it when war broke out, and never expected to see it again.

Turning, he began to walk away, blaming himself for not anticipating such an encounter—an encounter which, at that moment, was the last thing he wanted. After three years of war he had almost forgotten the man's existence; but it was apparent that the mechanic had not forgotten him. A quick glance over his shoulder revealed Budette on the quay, in pursuit.

Bertie quickened his pace, hoping to lose his pursuer

among the miscellaneous boats and fishing gear that lay strewn about in front of the tiny houses that backed the wharf—a wharf that had been reserved for the local people. He dare not run for fear of attracting the attention of people, men and women, who were standing about, some loitering, others working on their fishing tackle. But this reluctance did not apply to the mechanic, who broke into a trot, with the result that as Bertie was turning out of the wharf into the Place d'Armes he felt himself caught by the arm. Turning, he looked into the grinning face of François Budette, and knew that it was useless to pretend he did not know him.

'Bon jour, milord!' cried François. 'C'est bon! Je suis content . . .*'

Bertie stopped him with a word, and glancing along the wharf was relieved to see that the meeting appeared not to have been noticed by anyone.

'Have you been here all the time, milord?' asked François wonderingly.

'No,' Bertie told him. 'I have just returned. But let us not talk here. If I am caught by the police I shall be shot as a spy.'

François's face expressed concern. 'That is no use,' he muttered.

'No use at all,' agreed Bertie. 'Where can we talk?'

'There is still wine to be had in the Café de la Côte d'Azur—you remember the old place?'

'No, there are too many people,' broke in Bertie. 'I know it's no use trying to deceive you, so I shall have to tell you the truth. Let us find a place where it is quiet.'

* French: Good day, my Lord. This is good. I am pleased . . .

'Come home with me. My wife will be so glad to see again the English milord.'

Bertie thought swiftly. 'Yes, that's the best thing,' he assented.

'I still live in the same house,' remarked François, leading the way to one of the cottages behind the wharf.

'I see you've still got the old boat?'

'But of course. I take care of her. There is no petrol any more, but all the same I keep her good in case one day you come back.'

'I shall remember that, François,' returned Bertie. 'Do you still use the boat?'

'*Oui*. The Italians gave me a fishing licence, so I fix a sail to catch the lobsters by Cap Martin. But without the petrol, the boat is not so fast as when we won the Grand Prix, milord. My God! That was a race to remember. Those were the days.' The mechanic glanced around. 'How goes the war, do you think?' he asked in a low voice. 'Shall we win?'

'Who do you mean by we?'

'The British and the Americanos. Every day we pray for them, milord.'

'You prefer the good old days, eh?'

François indicated the town with a sweep of his brown arm. 'Look at the place. It falls to pieces. No money, no food, except fish and potatoes—and not many potatoes. There is not coffee any more, and the bread she is black. Everyone goes broke. Even the casino goes broke. These Nazis stay at the hotels but they do not pay. The Italians take everything. They do not, like the English, understand what it is to be sporting—no. *Tiens!* These are bad times.'

François turned through a tangle of fishing gear into a neat little house with bright green doors and shutters.

An elderly woman, fat, swarthy as an Indian, glanced up from the stove over which she was bending. Her back straightened. She uttered a cry of glad surprise. 'The milord!'

Bertie held out his hand. '*Bon jour*, Madame Budette.'

Madame shook his hand warmly, looking from one man to the other. 'But this is something I do not understand!' she cried.

'Shut the door, *mon vieux**, and I will tell you why I am here,' answered Bertie.

François closed the door, pulled forward a chair, and took a bottle from the cupboard. 'A glass of cognac, milord?' he offered.

'Not just now, thanks,' declined Bertie. 'I have things to do. Where are the children, *madame?*'

'At school.'

'Good. I must go before they return or perhaps they will chatter with their friends and so bring the police here. In any case I will not stay long because you are risking your lives by having me in your house. I tried to run away from François, but he caught me, and here I am.'

'Where have you come from, milord?' asked François.

'I have come,' replied Bertie, 'from England.'

François gasped. '*Nom de Dieu!* But how?'

'By aeroplane.'

'But why?'

'I am looking for a friend. But if the Italians catch me they will shoot me for a spy.'

'A friend!' François' eyes narrowed. '*Tiens!*' he

* French: my old friend

breathed. 'Then you are perhaps a friend of the Englishman who all the police are looking for?'

Bertie's face flushed with excitement. 'Then he is still alive?'

Madame shrugged. 'Who knows? All we know is, an Englishman was here. He came, it is said, to fetch a girl who was locked up at the *poste de police**, on the Rock. There was shooting here, and on *La Grande Corniche*. That is all we know. After that we are told not to mention the affair, but so many police came we think he got away. Nobody knows anything for certain. Where do you stay while you are in Monaco, milord?'

'Nowhere in particular.'

'Then you will stay with us,' invited François.

Bertie smiled. 'No, my friends, thank you all the same. This is no affair of yours. All I ask is, forget that you saw me here, or you may find yourselves in serious trouble.'

'But you must eat, milord,' muttered *madame*, with a worried frown.

'I shall manage.'

'Have some of my soup now? It is good.'

'That is an invitation I will not refuse,' declared Bertie.

Madame bustled about laying the meal.

'What I do not understand is, how do you expect to find your friend?' said François. 'Where will you look for him? In the casino? In the museum? Will he walk along the Boulevard des Moulins, or sit on the terraces? But no! This is not possible with the place so full of police.'

'First, I am going to look for some writing on a wall.'

* French: the police station

71

'On what wall, milord?'

'The wall behind the Quai de Plaisance.'

François slapped his thigh and clicked his tongue. '*Zut alors!* Now, here is a thing the most curious,' he exclaimed. 'One day I saw a girl writing on that very wall. She wore a blue shawl, I remember.'

Bertie stared. 'What day was this?'

François twisted his face in an effort to think. '*Oh la la.* I forget. It was many days ago—seven—eight—perhaps ten—I do not know. All days are the same here.'

'What did she write?'

'Fool that I am, I did not look. When I saw her writing I was working in the boat. I think when I go home I will look what she writes, but the sun is hot and I forget.'

Bertie looked from one to the other. 'I know nothing of such a girl,' he said. 'If she was writing, then it is no concern of mine. Just where did it happen?'

'This side of the Escalier du Port. There was a young man standing there this morning, a seller of onions, on the very spot. Perhaps you noticed him?'

'Er—yes—er—a man selling onions.'

'Is there anything remarkable in that?'

Bertie hesitated, but only for a moment. 'He, too, is my friend. He is helping me find the one who is lost.'

François started for the door. 'I go to see if there is writing on the wall.'

'No,' protested Bertie. 'I'll go.'

'It is better that I should go. Everyone knows me. You eat your soup, milord. *Au revoir.*'

Bertie turned to *madame*. 'It is nearly time for the children to come home?'

Madame nodded. 'I will go to the convent and tell

them that to-day they must eat with their aunt who lives in the Avenue Bellvue. They shall remain until I fetch them, this evening. It is better so.'

'*Merci madame.* It is good of you to go to so much trouble.'

'Do not speak of it, milord.' Madame hurried off on her errand.

About ten minutes later François returned. His face was flushed with excitement. 'There is writing, in the colour blue,' he said in a tense voice.

'What does it say?'

'It just says, Chez Rossi. Pernod. There is also a little mark.'

'A triangle.'

'*Exactement!**'

Bertie looked puzzled. 'Chez Rossi? What is this place—a restaurant?'

'Yes. It is at the back of the town, next to the Escalier des Revoires. But it is not a good place, I've heard tell.'

'What's wrong with it?'

'Mario Rossi, the owner. He is Italian, and that is not all. It is said . . .' François dropped his voice to a whisper. 'It is said he is a Camorrista**. They are too handy with their knives. The Chez Rossi is no place for a gentleman like you.'

'All the same,' declared Bertie. 'I must go.'

'What will you do there?'

'I shall look for something with the mark Pernod— a bottle perhaps.'

'Let me go,' offered François. 'It will be safer. Me,

---

* French: exactly
** A member of the Camorra

I am known to everyone in the town, but you, milord, if the police see you too much they may ask questions. Stay here and rest. I will find out what I can. The people here will not talk to strangers, but they will talk to me. I shall hear the latest rumours of this affair of the Englishman and the girl.'

Bertie perceived the wisdom of his advice. As a native François would be able to ask questions more or less with impunity. At any rate, he stood a much better chance of gathering information than a stranger.

'I accept your offer, François,' he decided. 'But be careful how you ask questions.'

'Leave that to me,' said François confidently. 'You rest here. *Au revoir*, milord.'

Left alone, Bertie settled down to make up for the rest he had lost during the night. He did not hear *madame* return, but it was getting dark by the time François came back.

'Well, old lobster, what did you discover?' asked Bertie.

'Not much,' replied François, looking crestfallen. 'I could see nothing of Pernod. I spoke to Mario and asked him if he knew of any blue writing, or of anything to do with Pernod. He said no, he knew of no such thing, but I do not trust the fellow. He gave me a queer look when I mentioned blue writing. It is my opinion that he knows more than he says. I asked him if any strangers had been there, and he said no; but his woman told me that a stranger, a young Spanish seller of onions had been in. That makes Mario a liar straight away. After that I went round the cafés trying to hear news of the English spy the people are talking about, but no one knows anything, except that the police have had orders to keep their mouths shut. That's all.'

'Thank you, *mon vieux*. Only one thing is clear. My friend the onion-seller has read the writing on the wall, and he followed the clue to the Chez Rossi. I wonder where he went after that?'

François shook his head. 'I don't know. I saw nothing of him.'

Glancing through the little window Bertie saw that night had fallen. 'I think I'll go and have a look round myself,' he said. 'It should be safe enough now it is dark.'

'And you will come back, milord?'

Bertie picked up his guitar. 'Perhaps—if I need a friend. Here, take this, and get some food, in case I come back hungry.' As he spoke Bertie took out some money and passed it to the mechanic. François would have refused it, but Bertie insisted. 'It is in the interest of everyone,' he said. '*Au revoir*, François. *Au revoir, madame.*'

'*Au revoir, monsieur.*'

Bertie went out into the night.

He walked along to the Quai de Plaisance, and in the light of his torch examined the writing to confirm that François had not overlooked anything. He was puzzled about the reference to the girl, but not seeing how she could fit into the scheme of things he dismissed her from his mind, and made his way, slowly, for he had sometimes to stop and ask the direction, to the bar-restaurant at the corner of the Escalier des Revoires. He went in, sat at a table and glanced around. There was perhaps a dozen customers, mostly at the bar, talking in low tones. A woman was serving. She came over to him.

'*Monsieur?*'

'The soup,' ordered Bertie.

'*Oui, monsieur.*'

As the woman was turning away Bertie asked casually, 'Where is Mario to-night?'

'He has had to go out for a little while on business,' replied the woman, and went on to the kitchen, to return presently with the soup.

Bertie ate it slowly, watching the people around him, but he could detect nothing suspicious in their actions. He had nearly finished, and was thinking of leaving, when he was startled by hearing shots in the distance. The other customers stopped talking to listen, and then, as there were more occasional shots, went to the door, guessing in quick excited voices what it might be.

'I should say,' said one, 'they have at last tracked down the Englishman.'

Nobody disputed this, and as the subject was not pursued, Bertie went out. But instead of leaving the district he turned in the bottom of the *escalier* from where he could see the front and side entrances of the restaurant—practically the same spot on which Ginger had stood only a short time before.

There was no more shooting, and soon afterwards the men went back into the bar. Bertie moved deep into shadow and leaned against a wall. He was not expecting anything unusual to happen, and his chief reason for remaining was, he thought he might as well, for he had nowhere else to go unless he returned to François.

Five minutes passed. Then he heard swift footsteps approaching, and a second later a man turned the corner. He went straight to the side entrance of the Chez Rossi. For a moment or two while he stood there, one foot on the step, listening, the light from the kitchen window illuminated a dark, swarthy face. He was breathing heavily, and his nostrils were quivering, dilated, as though with excitement. Then he went in, closing the door behind him.

Bertie guessed that the new arrival was Mario Rossi, and the man's obvious agitation so aroused his curiosity that he went over to the kitchen window in the hope of learning the explanation. There was a muslin blind drawn over the lower part of the window, but this did not prevent him from getting a fairly clear view of the interior of the lighted room. The man whom he assumed to be Mario was there, and his actions were now even more sinister than they had been outside.

First, he took from his pocket a red-stained handkerchief and threw it into the stove. Then, going quickly to the sink, he rinsed his hands, and Bertie noticed that the water which fell from them was also red. This done, he wiped his hands on a towel, examined his clothes for some reason that was not apparent, put on an apron, and lit a cigarette with hands that trembled so violently that he had difficulty in making match and cigarette meet. For a few seconds he drew at the cigarette in short, nervous whiffs, but this evidently did little to steady his nerves, for, crossing to a cupboard, he took down a bottle and helped himself to a generous drink.

He had just replaced the bottle when the woman who had been serving in the bar came in. Bertie could not hear what was said, but the woman's face expressed surprise. The man said something, and turning on his heel, opened a door and disappeared up a narrow flight of stairs. The woman filled some plates with soup and went back into the restaurant.

Bertie stood back, trying to work out what all this meant. From what he had seen, there was good reason to suppose that something unpleasant had happened. He felt certain that the stains on Mario's handkerchief and hands were blood. The question was, whose blood? He remembered what François had said about the man being a member of the notorious Italian secret society, the Camorra, and he knew that the methods of the Camorra were deadly, that the usual weapon was the stiletto*; but even so, he found it hard to believe that the man could just have committed a murder. Such things rarely happen. Yet, reflected Bertie, Mario's manner certainly suggested that something of the sort had happened.

He hung about for a bit, and then, as there was no development, without any definite object in view he strolled down towards the town. Somewhat to his surprise he met François coming up, and his surprise turned to alarm when François grabbed him by the arm and he saw the expression on his face. It was clear that the old mechanic was the bearer of hot news, and his first words conveyed the extent of its importance.

'*Mon Dieu!* Praise the saints that I have found you.'

'What has happened?' asked Bertie tersely.

'Haven't you heard?'

'No.'

'There has been a murder, a stabbing.'

'What of it? I didn't do it.'

'No, but your friend did.'

'What!' Bertie's voice was brittle with incredulity. 'Ridiculous!'

François shrugged. 'Perhaps. But this is certain. All the police in the town—and there are many— are hunt-

---

* A narrow, razor-sharp knife

ing for the young Spanish seller of onions. He was in the room with the body—they saw him leave.'

'Whose body?'

François looked furtively to left and right. 'The body of Gaspard Zabani, of the Villa Valdora.'

Chapter 6
Strange Encounters

There was a short silence during which Bertie stood and stared blankly at his informant.

'I still say it's nonsense,' he declared. 'We don't carry daggers.'

François threw out his hands appealingly. 'But, milord, the police find onions under the window by which the assassin entered. I tell you the police are turning the principality inside out in their search for him. And, what is more, there is a rumour going round that these onions are not Spanish, but English onions.'

Bertie tried to get the thing in line. 'How did you hear of this?'

''*Cre Dieu*! Everyone knows. First there was the shooting.'

'Yes, I heard that,' admitted Bertie.

'That was the police shooting at the assassin as he ran. Afterwards I stand in a doorway and listen to some police talking. They say that there was no reason for a Spaniard to kill Zabani, but plenty of reason why an Englishman should. Zabani, when he saw death coming, knocked over the telephone, and with his last breath called the police. They came at once, while the assassin was still there. He ran. They fired—*bang*—*bang*! They wounded him.'

Bertie felt his muscles contract. 'Wounded him?' he echoed, aghast.

'Yes. He fell, but ran on, leaving a trail of blood.

Voila! The blood leads down an *escalier*, but stops suddenly in the Place d'Armes. There the police lost track of him, but they think he is still in La Condamine. There was much blood. He could not get far, they say.'

'By Jove! This is awful,' muttered Bertie. His brain was whirling.

'Zabani was one of the richest men in the principality,' offered François.

Bertie did not answer. He wanted to think. He realized that it was quite on the boards that Ginger might have gone to the house of the man who had betrayed the princess. Could he have killed Zabani in self-defence?

François' next words swept the suspicion aside. 'It was a crime of revenge,' said he.

'How do you know that?'

François pulled Bertie's head forward and breathed in his ear. 'It was the knife of a Camorrista. The dagger carried the usual sign, a letter C, on a piece of paper.'

'My God!' whispered Bertie, suddenly seeing daylight. In the shock of François' information he had forgotten Mario.

'Was your friend of the Camorra?' asked François nervously.

'No,' snapped Bertie.

'Pardon, milord.'

'François,' said Bertie in a hard voice, 'did you tell me that Mario Rossi was a Camorrista?'

'But yes—so they say.'

'He killed Zabani.'

'How could you know this, milord, when you did not even know there had been a killing?'

'Listen! A few minutes ago Mario came running back to the restaurant, to the side entrance. Watching through the window, I saw him wash blood from his hands. His handkerchief, also bloodstained, he threw in the fire.'

François whistled softly through his teeth.'*Tiens*! The affair becomes *fantastique*.'

'No,' denied Bertie. 'I begin to see the way of it. *Attendez**! My friend, the one whom you call the British spy, must have known something of this man Mario, which is why he wrote the name of the restaurant on the wall of the Quai de Plaisance. There is another link between my friend and this man Zabani. My other friend, the onion seller, is also concerned.' Bertie broke off. The fact was, he felt that he held the pieces of a jigsaw which, could he but fit them together, would present a complete picture and so solve his problem. 'I must find the onion seller,' he decided.

François threw up his hands. '*Comment*?** If the police cannot find him, how can you hope to do so? He has gone into hiding, no doubt—but where?'

Bertie saw the sense of François' argument. It was not much use walking about the streets of Monaco without a clue of any sort, trying to find Ginger.

'There is one thing I can do,' he predicted.

'What is that?'

'See Mario Rossi.'

'Name of a dog! Are you mad, milord? If he has done one murder he will do another. These Camorrista, they use a dagger like we use a toothpick.'

'Nevertheless, I will go,' asserted Bertie. 'Time presses, and I am no use at guessing. Perhaps I can make Mario talk.'

---

* French: Wait!
** French: How?

'It is more likely, I think, that he will cut your throat.'

'Listen, *mon ami**,' went on Bertie. 'For the time being you go your own way. Gather what news you can of this affair. If all goes well with me you will see me to-morrow on the Quai de Plaisance.'

'Very well, milord. It was always said that you were mad. Now I believe it, too. *Adieu***.'

'*Au revoir*, and thanks for your help. One day, when the world becomes sane again, we will laugh over this affair.'

With a wave Bertie turned away and walked back to the Chez Rossi. He went straight to the side of the building and peered through the window into the kitchen. Mario was there, in an apron and white chef's cap, cooking something over the stove.

Bertie opened the door and went in. The Italian heard the movement and whirled round. His eyebrows went up. 'You have come to the wrong entrance,' said he, speaking in French. 'The bar is at the front of the house.'

Bertie smiled, and answered in the same language. 'No, I have come to the right entrance. I want to talk to you.'

'I have no money for beggars.'

'I am not looking for money.'

'Then what are you looking for?'

'A friend.'

'How can I help you?'

'You can help me,' said Bertie distinctly, 'by telling me why you killed Gaspard Zabani.'

* French: My friend
** French: Goodbye

83

Mario, who had half turned back to his stove, spun round as though he had been stung. 'Kill who?' he demanded in a thin, hard voice. 'I never killed a man in my life.'

Bertie stroked the strings of his guitar. 'Oh, yes, you have, my friend. You killed Zabani to-night. For that swine I don't care a broken guitar string. All I want to know is why you did it, because that may help me to find my friend.'

For nearly a minute the Italian stared at Bertie, his face distorted with passion. 'I tell you I know nothing of any murder,' he grated. 'Who are you—the secret police?'

Bertie shook his head. 'No. The police are looking for a young Spanish seller of onions. They think he killed Zabani, but I know better.'

Mario drew a deep breath that might have meant relief. 'I have seen this Spaniard,' he asserted. 'He came here for lunch.'

'Was that all?'

'As far as I know.'

'What did he drink with lunch—Pernod?'

Bertie knew, from the nervous twitch of the man's nostrils, that his shot had found its mark.

'No, he did not drink Pernod,' spat Mario spitefully. As he spoke his eyes flashed for an instant to the side of the room.

The unconscious movement had not been lost on Bertie, who was watching the man closely. His eyes went to the spot, and he saw, near the floor, half pushed behind a cupboard, what was evidently a show-card. One half only was visible, but it was enough to tell him what it was, for the standard advertisement for Pernod is on every hoarding in France.

84

'You are not a good liar, Mario,' he said coldly, and walked over to the card. He stooped to pick it up. As his fingers closed over it the world seemed to explode inside his head in a sheet of orange flame, and he knew that Mario had struck him. The flame faded slowly to purple, and then to black. He pitched forward on his face and lay still.

Chapter 7
Good Samaritans

When Bertie opened his eyes the flickering fingers of another day were sweeping upward from the eastern horizon to shed a mysterious light on the ancient Principality of Monaco. Somewhere near at hand palm fronds began to stir, rustling among themselves.

For a little while he lay still, trying to remember what had happened. With an effort he sat up, only to bury his face in his hands in a vain attempt to steady the throbbing in his head. Slowly, as full consciousness returned, and with it the memory of the blow that had struck him down, he looked about him, and saw that he was on a landing half-way down a steep flight of stone steps. On one side a cliff rose sheer. In it there was a little niche occupied by the statue of a saint, surrounded by tinsel and artificial flowers. On the other side a gorge fell sheer for two hundred feet to a tiny church that had been built in the bottom. He recognized it instantly, and knew that he was on the Escalier Ste. Dévote. How he had got there he did not know, but he supposed that Mario, after striking him down, had either carried him or thrown him there, perhaps imagining that he was dead. His head ached, and he felt bruised in several places, but as far as he could discover he had suffered no serious injury. The guitar lay beside him.

A woman came hurrying down the steps with a bowl of water and a towel.

'Poor man,' she said. 'I saw you from my window above. They are dangerous, those steps; you were lucky you did not go right over into the gorge. Doubtless the good Sainte Dévote saved you—all praise to her.'

'Doubtless,' murmured Bertie.

The woman bathed his head where the hair was wet and sticky. 'The least you can do after this escape is to offer a candle or two in our little church of Ste. Dévote,' she suggested.

'Candles shall indeed be lighted,' returned Bertie fervently, beginning to suspect that Mario had intended he should go into the gorge, in which case every bone in his body must have been broken.

'There,' said the woman. 'I don't think your skull is cracked, but if I were you I would rest for a little while.'

'A thousand thanks, *madame*,' answered Bertie, pulling himself to his feet. For a moment or two everything spun round him, but then steadied itself. 'Yes, I think I am all right,' he went on. 'I will rest on a seat on the Quai de Plaisance. I shall remember you, *madame*, in my gratitude.'

'A woman can do no less,' was the pious response. 'My little son fell in just the same way not long ago, and had it not been for Our Lady he must have been killed. Don't forget to give thanks.'

'You may be sure I shall not forget,' answered Bertie earnestly. 'My compliments to your husband, who is a lucky man to have a wife so sympathetic.'

The woman smiled. 'I must get back to my kitchen. *Adieu, monsieur.*'

'*Adieu, madame*, and thank you.'

The woman flung the bloodstained water in her bowl into the gorge and went off up the steps. Bertie, with his guitar under his arm, went down, and turned to where the little church faced across the harbour. A black-robed priest was just opening the doors.

'*Mon père**', said Bertie, taking a hundred-franc note from his pocket, 'this morning I had a fall on the *escalier* above, and nearly lost my life. It is my desire to buy two large candles as a thank-you offering.'

The priest smiled. 'Come in, my son. You look pale. Are you hurt?'

'Not much,' answered Bertie.

'Nevertheless, perhaps a small glass of cordial would help to restore the life which our Sainte Dévote undoubtedly saved.'

'I think that would be a very good idea, father,' agreed Bertie, who was more shaken than he was prepared to admit.

Ten minutes later, in broad daylight, feeling well enough to be angry with the man who had struck him down, he crossed the road and made his way along the Quai de Plaisance. It was deserted except for a young girl dressed in the sombre habit of the true Monégasque. When he first saw her she was strolling up and down as though waiting for someone, but when she noticed him, without altering her gait she began at once to move towards him—or so it seemed to Bertie, although he did not think this could really be the case.

Reaching the seat for which he had been making, he sat down to wait for Algy, or possibly Ginger. It was time, he decided, to discuss things with them. He wasn't even thinking about the girl, but he glanced up at her as she drew level. To his amazement—for the girls of Monaco are celebrated for their modesty—she

* French: My father

88

made a movement with her head that said as plainly as words that she wanted him to follow her. Had it not been for the faint flush that rose to her olive cheeks as she did this he would have ignored the signal, thinking that he had been mistaken. As it was, he half rose, and then, embarrassed, sank down again.

The girl strolled back, passed him, meeting his eyes squarely. She turned again, now walking back towards the Condamine. As she passed the bench she said quietly but distinctly, in English, 'Please follow me, *monsieur*, but do not speak. Eyes may be watching.'

She walked on, more quickly now, without once looking back.

Bertie, not a little surprised, picked up his guitar and followed. Straight along the avenue of oleander trees that fringes the Boulevard Albert, where policemen stood at intervals, walked the girl in black, with Bertie at a reasonable distance behind. She crossed the Place d'Armes, where more police were standing near some ugly stains on the ground, and took the long ramp that leads from the harbour to the top of the rock on which the old village of Monaco has sat in the sun for two thousand years or more. Reaching the top, she crossed the front of the palace and turned into a narrow street where tall stone houses threw a welcome shade.

When Bertie reached the entrance she was standing at the doorway of a private house. With a slight inclination of her head she disappeared. Reaching the spot, Bertie looked with suspicion into a hall so dark that for a moment he could see nothing. Was this, he wondered, a trap? Then he made out a pale oval face just inside.

'Enter, *monsieur*,' said a soft, sweet voice. 'A friend awaits you.'

Bertie went in and the girl closed the door.

'This way, *monsieur*,' she said, and ascended a flight of stairs. A door was opened, allowing bars of white sunlight to blaze across the corridor. Bertie stepped forward and looked into the room. In a high four-poster bed, his face nearly as pale as the counterpane, but smiling, lay Ginger.

'Good lord!' exclaimed Bertie.

Ginger's smile broadened. 'Come in,' he invited.

A voice at Bertie's elbow said quietly, 'The patient is a little weak from loss of blood, that's all. He wanted to get up, but we thought it better that he should rest for a while. You will be quite safe here, *monsieur*.' The girl went out and closed the door.

'Isn't she a wizard?' were Ginger's first words, rich with enthusiasm.

'Who?'

'Jeanette.'

'Just a minute, old boy,' protested Bertie. 'What is this? Where are we? What's going on?'

Ginger raised his eyebrows. 'Do you mean to say you don't know whose house you're in?'

Bertie sat on the edge of the bed. 'How should I know?'

'I thought Jeanette would tell you. I asked her to go to the Quai de Plaisance to see if you were there—a thin bloke with a guitar.'

'But who is this damsel?' demanded Bertie.

'Jeanette Ducoste—Henri's sister. He called her his little sister, but I reckon she's grown a bit since he went off to the war. This is number six, Rue Marinière.'

Bertie exploded. 'Well, I'm dashed! How did you get here?'

'That,' answered Ginger, 'is a longish story. I did a

spot of housebreaking and got plugged in the leg—I'm all right now, though; just a bit weak, that's all. I thought it was about time we compared notes.'

'I've got a few things to tell you, my lad,' declared Bertie. 'I'm not so bright myself. An Italian waiter walloped me on the boko last night, and the old skull still rocks a bit.'

Before Ginger could answer there came a sharp knock on the door below. Up the stairs came the sound of voices. A moment later the bedroom door was opened quietly and Jeanette entered. Her face was pale.

'What is it, Jeanette?' asked Ginger quickly.

Jeanette moistened her lips. 'It is the police,' she whispered. 'Mama is talking to them at the door.'

Chapter 8
Jock's Bar

When Algy had elected to go to Nice he knew that he had a long walk ahead of him; it seemed a good twelve miles. One thing in his favour was the gradient, which, between La Turbie and Nice, drops nearly two thousand feet to sea level. Even so, it was a weary walk. Some of the views were magnificent even in the moonlight, the sea on one hand and mountain peaks on the other, but with the fate of Biggles weighing heavily on his mind he was in no mood to appreciate them. He was relieved when, at last, at a bend of the road, after tramping for about three hours, he saw the wide panorama of Nice, the Brighton of the Riviera, before him.

During the entire journey he saw only four persons, and all were police. His role was well tested. First he ran into a *poste*. Two men were on duty. They accepted his story of being a repatriated French soldier, bound for Nice, and allowed him to pass. Then he was stopped by a patrol of two more police. Much the same thing happened. He produced the papers provided by Air Commodore Raymond, and after a short examination was permitted to proceed. From these experiences he observed that the police were on the alert, more so than normal circumstances seemed to warrant. He suspected that the extra vigilance was the result of the Biggles affair.

By the time he had descended the long hill leading down to the town, lights were beginning to appear, and a few early risers were moving about the streets. From the clock on the casino in the Place Massena he learned that it was half-past four. There was nothing he could do in the dark, so, turning up his collar, he found a seat in the public gardens opposite the jetty, and managed to get in a nap. He was awakened by the calls of a boy selling newspapers.

He turned down his collar, shook himself, and walked to the sea-wall, where began the famous Promenade des Anglais, a splendid esplanade stretching for several miles. He had no idea where Jock's Bar was situated, or who Jock was, or whether the bar was open. He soon discovered that there were cafés and sun-bathing establishments at intervals all along the promenade. These premises, locally called bars, were not actually on the promenade, but under it, being approached by steps leading down to the beach. The name of each bar was advertised by a painted sign. Looking down over the railings at the first one, which carried the name Ruhl Plage, he saw that it was not so much a bar as a bathing beach; not that it mattered, because the shutters were up and the place was obviously closed, presumably for the duration of the war. The beach was deserted. It was the same with the second, and the third, which turned out to be his objective, the notice 'Jock's Bar' being prominently displayed in sun-faded letters. Walking down the stone steps that led to the beach and the café, he saw that the place, like the rest, was shuttered. Not only was it closed, but high seas during the preceeding winter had flung tons of shingle over what had evidently been a concrete sun-bathing 'apron', and against the door. In fact, stones were piled along the whole front; some of them had been hurled so high and with such force by the waves, that the shutters were broken. It was obviously an ideal place for the purpose for which Biggles had proposed to use it, because, in the first instance, few people would be likely to pass along the front of it, and secondly, there were plenty of convenient places on which to write.

Algy made his way slowly along the frontage. As he walked he scrutinized the wall and the boarding for writing; at the same time he kept one eye, so to speak, on the railings above, in case any person looking down from the promenade should see him and wonder what he was doing.

Almost at once he came upon what he hoped to find—writing in blue pencil. There was good reason to suppose that it would be there, yet the sight of it made his nerves tingle with shock, perhaps because it was a definite link with Biggles. But as his eyes fastened on the writing he experienced a pang of disappointment. The message was brief—too brief to be of much use. It merely said *VILLA V*. This was followed by a swastika and this, in turn, by a blue triangle. There was nothing to indicate when the message had been written, although its purport was clear. Villa V obviously referred to the Villa Valdora. The swastika meant that it was occupied by the enemy. The triangle was, of course, Biggles' signature. With sinking hopes Algy realized that the message must have been written before the attempted escape from the Californie landing ground.

Satisfied that there was nothing more to be learned, he was about to retrace his steps when he saw something that at once held his attention. It was an ugly, dark-coloured smear, roughly the shape of a man's hand, on the sea-wall. It seemed to attract innumerable flies. A little farther along, just below a fracture in the shutter, there was a similar mark. Between them there were dark spots on the ground.

Algy stood still, everything else forgotten. He did not stop to reason out how he knew, but he was sure that the marks were bloodstains. He could think of nothing else that would cause the same marks – unless they had been made deliberately by a practical joker. He walked nearer to the shutter, and saw another stain on the edge of the woodwork.

With his heart thumping with excitement he went right up to the shutter and pushed the broken slats aside, making a gap wide enough for a man to enter. He looked in. It was like looking into a vault. All he could see was a dark-grey concrete chamber backed by a row of doors bearing numbers, evidently bathing cabins. In the dim light it all looked grim, cold and damp. Just inside lay what looked like a bloodstained piece of rag.

Algy climbed through. He did not know precisely what he was going to do; he had not thought as far ahead as that; but every instinct urged him on, and he knew that he could not go away without exploring the place. One thing was certain. A wounded man had been there. There was no proof that it was Biggles, but since he had named the place as a rendezvous, there was a chance that it might be. Such were Algy's thoughts—a trifle chaotic—as he climbed through the gap and stood on the concrete floor. Instantly he was seized by both arms.

For a moment he struggled, and then, seeing the men who seized him, he desisted. One was a short, dark, stockily-built man in civilian clothes. The other was a French *gendarme*.

'What's the matter?' demanded Algy indignantly in French, aware that he had blundered into a trap.

'What are you doing here?' demanded the civilian.

'I was going to undress and have a bathe,' declared Algy. 'Is there anything wrong with that?'

'Let me see your papers.'

'Who are you?'

'My name is Signor Gordino. You may have heard of me. I am head of the special police.'

'I beg your pardon, sir,' answered Algy, affecting humility. He produced his identity papers and passed them over.

The civilian examined them closely—in fact, so minutely that Algy realized that he was in a tight corner. He remembered what Air Commodore Raymond had said about Gordino.

'I am not satisfied with these,' said the Italian.

'Why not? What sort of treatment is this? I am a French citizen,' asserted Algy hotly.

'And I am Gordino,' was the curt response. 'Turn out your pockets.'

Now this was something Algy dare not do, for in one pocket he carried a torch, and in the other a British service automatic. The situation, he perceived, was so desperate that only desperate measures could meet it.

'Very well,' he said quietly, and put his hand in the pocket that carried the pistol. He took it by the squat muzzle, and drawing it swiftly, slammed it against the Italian's head. Almost with the same movement he kicked the *gendarme*'s legs from under him. The man fell, dropping his *bâton*. Algy snatched it up and, as the man started to scramble to his feet, struck him on the head with it. No second blow was needed. The man collapsed and lay still. The Italian was on his knees, one hand to his head.

Algy pocketed his pistol, dropped the *bâton*, snatched up his papers, which the Italian had dropped, and scrambled through the window into the bright sunlight. Panting with suppressed excitement, he ran on to the stone steps and so up to the promenade. This he crossed, and dived into a narrow street. He dare not run, for there were now a good many people about and he did not want to call attention to himself. He was well up the street when he heard a whistle blowing behind him.

His objective now was to get out of what was, or soon would be, a red-hot danger zone, as quickly as possible. He was no longer concerned with Jock's Bar because quite obviously, Biggles was not there. The only reason for remaining in Nice was to ascertain if the Californie landing ground was still serviceable. He would have preferred to postpone this investigation, but he saw clearly that after what had happened his only chance of doing it was immediately, before the hue and cry for him became general. Henri had said that Californie was about three miles to the west of Nice, on the way to Cap d'Antibes, so, turning to the left, he struck off along a wide boulevard that ran parallel with the sea front.

A workman came out of a yard wheeling a bicycle, and was about to mount when Algy, in whose head an idea had been born, strode up to him.

'My friend,' he said, 'I have most urgent reasons for getting to Californie. It is a matter of life or death. Walking is slow work. Will you sell me your bicycle?'

The man looked surprised. 'Why not take the Cannes autobus? It passes Californie.'

'How often does it run?'

'Every hour.'

'When is the next bus?'

The man looked at his watch. 'In half an hour.'

'That will be too late. Is it possible to buy a bicycle in the town?'

'There is a shop in the Avenue de la Victoire where they still have a few, but they are expensive.'

'That would mean going a long way back. How much will you take for yours?'

The man considered his machine. 'It is a good bicycle,' he observed.

This was a lie, for the bicycle was an old type, and badly worn, but Algy was in no mood to argue. 'How much?' he asked.

'I will sell you this very good bicycle for . . . a thousand francs.'

'In a matter of life or death money is of small importance,' answered Algy tritely, as he counted out the money. In another moment he was astride the saddle, pedalling down the road, leaving the late owner standing in the road, the notes in his hand, a look of wonder on his face.

Well satisfied with his bargain, Algy pedalled hard. He was anxious to get the business over, so that he could turn his back on Nice. As he sped down the road he tried to get into clearer focus the curious affair at Jock's Bar. One thing was certain. He had stepped into a trap. The police were there, waiting. For whom? Were they waiting for Biggles? If they were, then it meant that he was still alive. But why should they be waiting at Jock's Bar? Why should they suppose that he would go there? Certainly, something had happened there, for the bloodstains were there to prove it. Whose blood was it? Algy felt that if he knew the answer to that question it would provide the answer to a lot of things, but there seemed to be no way of finding out. Of course, he reasoned, he might be on the wrong track altogether. The stains, and the trap, might have no connection with Biggles. The whole thing might be coincidence. Doubtless there were other people wanted by the police in Nice besides Biggles.

With such thoughts as these surging through his brain, Algy came to Californie. A signpost told him that he had arrived, and a frayed windstocking on a crazy pole, on the left-hand side of the road, indicated the aerodrome. One glance told him all he needed to know. Men were at work with shovels throwing up heaps of stones. Two long rows of such obstruction had already been completed. They straggled right across the landing ground, making it useless for that purpose.

Algy was not unduly dismayed. He was half prepared for something of the sort. After all, it was an obvious precaution. He decided to make for Monaco forthwith to let the others know about it, and this decision was hastened by the appearance of two policemen at the door of a house not far away. Turning, he pedalled back to Nice. He would have avoided the town had it been possible, but it was not—unless he was prepared to make a detour of fifty or sixty miles through the mountains. He knew from the maps he had studied that three roads ran from Nice to Monaco, all close to each other, and more or less parallel with the coast. There was the *Grande Corniche*, over which he had walked during the night, the middle corniche and the lower corniche, which was used chiefly by heavy commercial traffic. This latter road was the most attractive because, as it followed the beach, there were no hills, but this advantage was offset by the fact that in the event of trouble there could be no escape. On one side the cliffs rose sheer; on the other side was the sea. For this reason he decided on the middle road, from which, in emergency, he could get up to the top corniche, or down to the lower one.

He was some time getting through Nice, for keeping well away from the sea front he lost himself in the extensive suburbs. In the end he had to dismount to ask the way. This was in the poorer quarter of the town, where an open-air market was being held. All sorts of articles were offered for sale on stalls, and the sight of a second-hand clothes shop gave him another idea. For a hundred francs he acquired some faded blue workmen's overalls, and these he put on over his suit in case a description of him had already been circulated. For the same reason he bought one of the local wide-brimmed straw sun-hats. Well satisfied with the change, directed by the man from whom he had bought the clothes, he continued his journey, and was soon climbing the long hill that overlooks the fishing village of Villefranche.

From there his journey was uneventful until he came to Eze, an ancient village perched precariously on a pinnacle of rock. There, to his disgust, his front tyre burst. It was now noon. The sun was hot and he was tired and hungry; so, leaning his bicycle against a tree, he went into a little café and made a miserable meal of vegetable soup and dry bread—there was nothing else. Having finished, he was waiting for the waitress to come back to ask her if there was anywhere in the village where he could get his burst tyre repaired, when the sound of motor-cycles pulling up outside, followed by voices, took him to the window. He saw four *gendar-*

mes. They had dismounted and were looking at his bicycle. One called to a labourer, who was working in a garden, 'Where is the man who owns this bicycle?'

The man straightened his back and pointed. '*Voila! monsieur.* He went into the café.'

Chapter 9
The Girl in the Blue Shawl

Algy waited for no more. Whether the *gendarmes* were merely making casual inquiries, or whether they had learned of his bicycle transaction, he did not know. Nor did he intend to find out if it could be avoided. He could not leave by the front entrance without being seen, so he went through to the back. He found himself in a kitchen where a man and a woman were seated at a table, eating.

'Excuse me,' said Algy, and passed on to the back door. Reaching it, he turned, and said over his shoulder, 'If you forget that you have seen me you will be helping France. *Merci, monsieur et m'dame.*' He felt he had something to gain and nothing to lose by saying this, for if he had said nothing the people would certainly tell the *gendarmes* which way he had gone, whereas now they might hesitate to do so.

Closing the door behind him he was confronted by a spectacle that has been the admiration of many tourists. It took his breath away. Immediately in front of him a steep slope fell away for nearly two thousand feet into the sea. On this slope hundreds of olive trees turned their grey leaves to the sun. Here and there shone the darker green of figs, and trailing vines. Between them, wild lavender, thyme and juniper, covered the ground among the grey rocks. It was not a path he would have chosen, but he had no choice. He dropped over the garden wall and scrambled to the nearest olives, which he hoped would prevent him from being seen from above. It seemed likely that the police would spend some minutes in the village, which would give him a fair start.

The heat on the sun-baked slope, which faced due south, was terrific, and hundreds of flies drank freely from the beads of perspiration that trickled down his face. But he kept on, glad that his journey lay downward, not upward. For twenty minutes he continued the mad scramble, jumping from rock to rock, swinging from olive branch to vine; then, hearing no sound of pursuit, he paused to get his breath and take stock of his surroundings. Reaching for a bunch of wild grapes he thrust the whole thing into his mouth to quench his thirst, heedless of the juice that dripped down the front of his overalls.

If he was followed he knew nothing of it, which was not remarkable, for the jungle of semi-tropical trees and shrubs stretched for miles on either side of him. Having rested for a while he began a more cautious descent, now making for the bottom Corniche road, which appeared from time to time below like a short length of yellow ribbon as it rounded a shoulder of rock. He kept on for another hour, by which time he was about a hundred yards above the road, along which occasionally passed heavy lorries, and not a few *gendarmes* on cycles or motor cycles.

He was now in a quandary. It seemed certain that he could not hope to use any of the roads without being stopped and questioned; on the other hand, it was manifestly impossible for him to make his way through the tangle of shrubs, and masses of rock, to Monaco, a distance of about four miles by road, but considerably more if the swelling contours of the mountain slopes were followed. He decided that he would have to use the road, but to wait for darkness, when the chances of discovery would be reduced. So, finding a comfortable spot to relax, he lit a cigarette and settled down to wait for night, and at the same time give serious thought to the affair at Jock's Bar; not so much the writing on the wall, which told him little, as the existence of the police trap which, without any real evidence, he felt sure was in some way concerned with Biggles. But although he cogitated on the problem for hours, he could arrive at no definite conclusion. He hoped the others had learned something which would throw light on the mystery.

As darkness closed in he descended to the road and made his way towards Monaco, travelling slowly because he was taking no chances that could be avoided. He reconnoitred each bend before showing himself. Just before the point where the road swings round into the Place d'Armes he had a piece of luck. A lorry had broken down, and the driver was working—not very cleverly—on the engine. Algy gave him a hand, and finding a fault in the ignition, put it right. He did this in no spirit of human kindness, but in order to get a lift, which the man gave him willingly. A minute later, at the frontiers of France and the Principality of Monaco, he had the anxious experience of sitting talking to the driver while two *gendarmes*, one Monégasque and one French, searched the back of the vehicle before allowing it to pass.

'They seem pretty strict all of a sudden,' suggested Algy to his companion, fishing for information.

'It's all these spies about,' answered the man vaguely.

'For my part I think it's just rumour,' replied Algy carelessly.

'I'm not so sure of that,' answered the driver. 'It wasn't rumour that got the woman out of jail.'

'What woman?'

'An Italian, they say. I have a brother-in-law in the *gendarmerie**, and he told me on the quiet that it was an Englishman who got her out—and got shot for his pains.'

'He was killed, eh?'

'My brother-in-law didn't say that. He pretends to know a lot, but it's my opinion that he doesn't know as much as he makes out. Where do you want me to drop you?'

'At the end of the Boulevard Albert. I'm going to meet a friend on the Quai de Plaisance.'

'Here we are then.' The driver pulled up.

'What hour is it?'

'It must be eight o'clock.'

Algy got out. 'Many thanks.'

'Don't mention it. *Bon soir***.'

Algy walked across the quay which, in the light of the stars, he saw was deserted. This was disappointing, for he had hoped to find Bertie or Ginger there—perhaps both of them. It was too dark to examine the wall for writing without using his torch, which was almost certain to attract attention, so there was nothing he could do but find a seat and wait. Time passed—one hour, two hours . . . he lost count. Nobody came. Not a soul. The moon rose over the mountains, and still nobody came. He began to get worried. He could

* French: police station
** French: Good evening

105

not imagine what Bertie and Ginger were doing. Surely one of them would show up. He wanted desperately to see them, for he felt that he had come to the end of his own particular trail, and did not know where to start on a new one. In the end he waited all night, and saw not a soul.

Just before dawn, feeling tired and dispirited, he walked along the sea wall, and throwing off his clothes, had a swim in lieu of a wash. He dried himself on his overalls. By the time he had finished dressing it was beginning to get light, and he was strolling back to the wall in order to examine it for writing, when a girl appeared. She emerged from the bottom of the Escalier du Port, and began to walk slowly along the wall. Beyond the fact that she wore a blue shawl Algy barely noticed her—at least, not for a minute or two; and then it suddenly struck him that she was doing exactly what he himself was doing. At all events, she was walking slowly along the wall, staring at it as if in search of something. This struck him as odd, but even then it did not occur to him that she might be on precisely the same errand as himself.

He watched her curiously while she covered a distance of perhaps a hundred yards. His curiosity mounted when he saw her stop, take a swift pace forward, and start doing something on the wall. She appeared to be rubbing it. This struck him as an extraordinary thing for a girl to do at that hour of the morning. He could not imagine what she was doing. With his eyes still on her he sauntered on, not wishing to risk causing a scene by accosting her. But when he saw that she was actually writing his curiosity could no longer be contained, and he broke into a sharp walk. At that moment the girl glanced furtively up and down the quay. She saw him at once, as was inevitable. She stopped what she was doing, and walking quickly to the escalier, disappeared from view.

Algy walked briskly to the spot where she had been working, and then stopped in astonishment. There was writing on the wall, and it was blue. In fact, there was more than that. Something had been erased, or rather, scribbled over, as though a message had been made illegible. Just on the right of this scrawl had been written in blue pencil, CASTILLON. AU BON CUISINE*. MAYDAY.

For a full minute Algy stared at this extraordinary message which—there was no doubt of this in his mind—he had actually just seen written. Then he tore up the *escalier*. The girl in the blue shawl was not in sight. He raced to the top of the steps, looked left and right, but of the girl there was no sign. The only person in view was an old man cleaning the windows of the water company's offices.

Now it is one thing to sit quietly at home and work out a complex puzzle, but it is an entirely different thing to be suddenly confronted with an unexplainable event, and know exactly what to do. Algy did not know what to do—or rather, he wanted to do two things at once. He wanted to find the girl, and he wanted to re-read the message to make sure that it was actually there. He could not do both, so for a moment or two he did neither. He stood like a man bemused, gazing up and down the road, hoping that the girl would reappear. But in this he was disappointed. So, when she did not show up, he made his way down to the

* French: Castillon. Where the cooking is good.

107

quay and re-read the message. It was there all right. CASTILLON. AU BON CUISINE. MAYDAY.

In this cryptic message, only one word really meant anything. *Castillon* conveyed nothing at all. It might, thought Algy, be a man's name, or a place—in fact, it might stand for almost anything. *Au bon cuisine* was a little more comprehensive, but not much. It might refer to some particular kitchen, or a place of good cooking. But *MAYDAY*, that was different. To a layman it might not mean much—perhaps merely the first day of May; but to Algy, as an airman, the word had a profound significance. For Mayday, derived from the French '*m'aidez*,' meaning 'help me,' is the international distress signal of aircraft in grave danger and in need of assistance. So, not only was the message a cry for help, but the use of the word implied that the person was accustomed to the technicalities of aviation. Written in blue, the colour chosen by Biggles, it would be a coincidence indeed if the message had not been sent, if not actually inscribed, by him. True, there was no triangle, but the girl had departed in such haste that she might well have overlooked it, even if it had been her intention to make such a mark. Where the girl in the blue shawl fitted into the puzzle was not apparent. But that did not matter. The great thing was, the message had only just been written, which meant— unless an incredible coincidence had occurred—that Biggles was still alive, and needed help. The girl, who would hardly be likely to understand the use of the word *Mayday* unless she had been told, must be in touch with him. The more Algy thought about it the more certain he became that this was the only reasonable answer.

He regretted bitterly that he had not followed her,

but regrets being futile, he decided to walk the streets until he found her; but hearing a step behind him he turned to find himself being regarded by an extremely ugly man with a cast in one eye—a boatman, or a fisherman, judging by his clothes. His sudden appearance reminded Algy of something he had forgotten, the two people he had come to the quay to find—Bertie and Ginger. They had still not put in an appearance. Perhaps the boatman had seen something of them—or at any rate, Bertie, whose guitar made him conspicuous.

He addressed the man in French. 'Excuse me for troubling you, but have you seen a man on this quay carrying a guitar?'

The man regarded him stonily. He spat, with thoughtful deliberation, into the sea. 'No,' he said distinctly.

'Were you here yesterday?'

'I am always here.'

'And you did not see him—all day?'

The man's eyes half closed. 'I have said,' he rasped, 'I have not seen any man with a guitar.'

Algy did not press the question. 'I am a stranger in these parts,' he explained. 'Tell me, does the word Castillon mean anything to you?'

The man considered the matter. 'It may—and it may not,' he replied.

Algy perceived that he was not likely to learn much from this churlish fellow. He had one last try.

'Is it a place—a village, perhaps?'

'It was,' replied the man. 'Are you thinking of going there?'

'Yes.'

The man laughed. 'The cats will be pleased to see you,' he observed.

'Cats?' Algy began to think he was dealing with a madman. 'Is this a village of cats?' he queried.

The man nodded. He seemed to be enjoying a private joke. 'That's right—a village of cats. The cats eat the birds. You will be able to eat the cats.' Roaring with laughter the man turned towards a motor boat that was tied up to the quay.

Algy took a last look round. Then, deep in thought, he walked slowly up the steps of the Escalier du Port. Looking back from the top he could see no sign of Bertie or Ginger. Only a young girl in black was walking along the Quai de Plaisance.

Chapter 10
Shattering News

When Bertie and Ginger, in the bedroom at Number 6, Rue Marinière, heard the police at the door, they assumed, naturally, that they had been traced. Had there been any way of escape it is likely that Bertie would have taken it, but hastening to the window he found himself gazing down for a hundred feet or more on to a pile of jagged rocks. Definitely, there was no escape that way. Indeed, it seemed that there was nothing they could do.

Ginger's first thought was for Jeanette and her mother, who had taken him in and befriended him, for it seemed likely that if alleged spies were discovered on the premises they would find themselves facing a firing party as accessories.

'I'm sorry about this, Jeanette,' he said bitterly, taking her hand. 'I should not have come here. Nor should I have asked you to find my friend and bring him here.'

'You did quite right to come here, *monsieur*,' said Jeanette softly.

During this brief interval voices could be heard at the door, but the actual words could not be distinguished. The voices ended abruptly. A door was closed. Footsteps could be heard slowly ascending the stairs. Jeanette ran to the corridor, looked out and came back.

'It is Mama,' she said. 'The police have gone.'

Ginger could hardly believe his ears. He had quite

made up his mind that the house was about to be searched.

Madame Ducoste came slowly into the room. Nobody spoke. All eyes were on her face, which was as pale as death.

'*Messieurs*,' she said in a low voice. 'It is tragic news.'

'You mean—they know I came here?' said Ginger.

'No. The visit had nothing to do with you. It concerned Henri.'

'Henri?' cried Bertie, incredulously.

'*Oui, monsieur*. He has been caught. It seems that the night before last he flew to these parts, doubtless to look again on his home; but in returning his engine failed, and he crashed.'

Algy glanced at Bertie. 'Where did this happen, *madame*?'

'Just beyond Peille. Between Peille and Baudon.'

'Was he hurt?'

'Yes, but not badly. His head was cut, and for a time he was unconscious. They carried him to Peille, where a doctor attended him, and where he will remain until he is well enough for the police to take him to Nice.'

'And then, *madame*?'

'He will be tried as a traitor.'

'This is what the police told you?'

'*Oui, monsieur*. They came to inform me officially of his arrest, and to ask me if he had been here.'

'You told them no?'

'I told them the truth. He has not been here.'

'Yes, we know that, *madame*,' said Ginger quietly.

'You know? How do you know this?'

'Because we know the errand that brought him here. It was he who brought us to Monaco. His engine must have gone wrong soon after he started back for

England. I'm sorry now that I did not tell you this before, but it seemed cruel to burden you with anxiety. I thought it was better that you should not know that it was he who brought us here in case by any chance you were questioned by the police. Then you could tell the truth, saying that you knew nothing of him.' Ginger looked at Bertie. 'I told *madame* that we knew Henri as a pilot of the Fighting French,' he explained. 'I did not tell her that he brought us here.'

Madame Ducoste sank into a chair, tragedy written on her face. 'They will shoot Henri,' she said in a dull voice.

Bertie spoke. 'Do you know where he is, in Peille, *madame*?'

'In the sanitorium.'

'Is there a guard?'

'A *gendarme* remains always with him.'

Bertie looked at Ginger. 'I've been to this place, Peille. It's about six miles from La Turbie, as the crow flies, at the far end of the valley in which we landed. It sits on a ledge, in the mountains. The sanitorium is just this side of the village.' To *madame* he said, putting his hand on her shoulder, 'Don't give up hope. There is still time for us to do something.' Ginger had never seen him so serious.

'But what can you do?' asked Madame Ducoste, helplessly.

'Leave the matter in our hands,' answered Bertie. 'It is rash to make promises, but we do not desert our friends.'

'I am sure of that,' breathed Jeanette.

'Confound this wound in my leg . . .' began Ginger.

'How long is it going to take to get right?' asked Bertie.

113

'I think I could get about,' returned Ginger. 'I'm a bit weak, that's all. It was *madame*'s suggestion that I should rest for a day or two, and until this happened I was prepared to take her advice.'

'I will make some soup,' said *madame*, and went down to the kitchen.

'You had better go down, too, *mademoiselle*,' suggested Bertie. 'We would like to talk things over.'

Jeanette's eyes smiled at Ginger, and she followed her mother down the stairs.

'Now that's my idea of a girl,' declared Ginger. 'I'm absolutely crazy about her. She's the most marvellous thing. . . .'

'Here, I say, just a minute, old boy,' reproved Bertie. 'Keep your hand on the jolly old throttle or you'll be out of control before you know where you are. Things are complicated enough as it is; if you're going to start ordering bouquets and writing poetry. . . .'

'Okay—okay,' broke in Ginger. 'She speaks English jolly well, too. Before the war *madame* used to let apartments to English visitors.'

Bertie took out his monocle and turned a cold eye on his companion. 'I don't care if she speaks Greek, Arabic, Hindustani and Urdu. Is this a romance or a rescue? What I'm waiting to hear is, how did you come to get in this mess?'

In a few words Ginger told him what had happened. 'I don't know where this waiter Mario comes in,' he concluded, 'but he's in the party. Biggles must have gone to the Chez Rossi. Mario, of the Chez Rossi, kills the man who double-crossed the princess. That isn't coincidence. I followed him to the Villa Valdora and got landed with the murder. I was all in when I got here, and passed out on the floor. Jeanette and her mother were marvellous. . . .'

'You've said that before.'

'I shall probably say it again,' declared Ginger. 'They looked after me as if I was their own son. When I came round I told them as much as I dare—said I was an Englishman looking for a friend who had got stuck down here. I didn't say anything about Henri flying us down for reasons which you heard me explain. Anyway, if I had, one thing would have led to another, and I didn't want to say too much. Naturally, I wanted to let you know what had happened, so I asked Jeanette to go down to the Quai de Plaisance to look for a bloke with a guitar. She found you and brought you along. What have you been doing?'

Ginger's face was a picture while Bertie told his story, which, of course, explained the mystery of his being followed by the boatman, François. 'There's no doubt that it was Mario who stuck the stiletto into Zabani,' continued Bertie. 'As you say, somehow he is mixed up in this; the way he hid the Pernod card and bumped me on the boko when I tried to have a dekko at it proves that. He's a nasty piece of work. I'll resume the argument with him when I have time. Meanwhile, this is a bad business about Henri. Even if we could get him away it looks as though we're stuck on the Riviera for the duration.'

'Looks like it,' agreed Ginger moodily. 'We don't seem to have done much towards settling the mystery of Biggles either. We still don't know whether he's dead or alive. I wonder what Algy's up to? You say he went to Nice?'

'That was the idea.'

'Then all I can think is there must have been some

writing on the wall at Jock's Bar to keep him there, or he would have been back by now.'

While he was speaking Jeanette came back into the room with a tray. She glanced at Ginger. 'Did I hear you speak about writing on a wall, *monsieur?*' she inquired.

'Why, yes, *mademoiselle,*' replied Bertie, looking surprised. 'Do you know anything about it?'

'Only that I have seen writing on a wall.'

'Where?'

'By the Quai de Plaisance.'

Ginger flashed a glance at Bertie, then looked back at Jeanette. 'When?'

'This morning, when I wait for *monsieur* of the guitar.'

Bertie turned to Ginger. 'Did you say anything to Jeanette about the writing on the wall?'

'Not a word,' declared Ginger. 'Tell me, Jeanette, what did you see?'

Jeanette shrugged a shoulder. 'I saw writing.'

'But how? I mean—did you know it was there?'

'But no. What happens was this,' explained Jeanette. 'As I walk down the hill this morning at the early hour to seek *monsieur* of the guitar—'

'Call him Bertie—it's shorter.'

'*Oui, monsieur.* As I go to find Bertie I see a girl with a shawl blue. She does something to the wall. I think, what can a girl do so early with a wall, so as I walk I watch. A man, he comes. He goes near. *Voila*! Mademoiselle of the shawl blue runs up the Escalier du Port. Monsieur, he runs to the place where she does something to the wall. He is agitated. He runs up the *escalier*. He runs back, *tout de suite**. He speaks with Monsieur

---

* French: immediately

Budette, he of the one eye. Monsieur Budette, he goes home. What is this, I think. Everyone is going somewhere. While I wait for *monsieur* Bertie I go to the wall to see what happens that makes everyone run. I see writing. *C'est tout**.*'

'In blue pencil?'

'But yes. How did you know?'

'And it said, "Chez Rossi. Pernod." '

'But no.'

Ginger stared. 'But yes! I saw it myself.'

'Then you do not see what I see,' returned Jeanette definitely. 'First, there is a place where someone has wrote. It is covered with much scribbling. Then there is writing. It says—' Jeanette wrinkled her forehead in an effort to remember. 'Oh, yes. It says: Castillon. Au bon cuisine. Then there is a word I do not know. The day of May. No, May Day.'

Ginger stared. 'Wait a minute,' he said slowly. 'Are you sure of this?'

'But certainly.'

Ginger turned an amazed face to Bertie. 'Now, what do you make of that?'

'Looks as though fresh writing has been put on the wall since we were there.' Bertie turned to Jeanette. 'This girl in the blue shawl—have you seen her before?'

'I am so far away I do not know, but I think no.'

'Was there a mark after the writing—a triangle?'

'I see no triangles.'

'And the man who ran up the steps—what did he look like?'

'Ah, I see him closer.' Jeanette gave a brief description.

* French: That's all

117

'Algy, by thunder!' cried Ginger. 'He must have been on the spot, probably waiting for us, and actually saw the girl writing. I wonder where he went?'

Jeanette smiled. 'He has gone, *monsieur*, to Castillon.'

'You spoke to him?'

'*Non*—I do not speak with strange men.'

'Then how do you know where he went?'

'I told you he speaks to Monsieur Budette, he who watches always the little boat that belongs once to his English milord. I, too, speak with Monsieur Budette. He has a joke the most comical. A man, he says, has asked him the way to Castillon.'

'That's the name you said was written on the wall.'

'Of course.'

'What is this word, Castillon?'

'Castillon is a village, *monsieur*. That is what is so droll.' Jeanette smiled again.

'What's funny about it?'

'No one is there, except cats, and, it is said, the ghosts.'

'Jeanette, please be serious,' pleaded Ginger. 'This is very important.'

'Pardon, *monsieur*, but I speak the truth.'

'Tell me about Castillon.'

'It is a village deserted, *monsieur*, in the mountains behind Mentone, fifteen kilometres, perhaps, from Monaco. I walk there once, with my brother Henri, for a *pique-nique**. It sits in a *col*—how you say? A gorge of the most steep, like a cut in the mountains. It is, to look at, like a heap of grey bones. You see, *monsieur*, one day long ago, when my father is a young man, there is an earthquake, and many of the houses fall

* French: picnic

down. The people are so afraid they run, they run all the time; they do not stop running until they come to Mentone. They do not go back—never. So the village it remains as it was left. Only the cats stay, many cats, which makes it the more desolate. That is why Monsieur Budette thinks it is a great joke for a man to go there.'

'Thank you, Jeanette.' Ginger looked at Bertie. 'Now we're getting somewhere. If the message is to be believed, someone is in need of help at this quaint village. It might be Biggles.'

'But who is this girl in the blue shawl?'

'How do I know? We'll find out. Let's get along. Algy is already on the way.'

'But you're in no case to go climbing about mountains.'

'There must be a path. Is there a path, Jeanette?'

'Yes, *monsieur*.'

Bertie broke in. 'But you're not fit enough—'

'I'm feeling fine,' declared Ginger. 'A bit weak, that's all. I can't lie here with all this going on.'

'What about Henri?'

'We shall have to do something about that, too.'

'Your soup will be cold, *messieurs*,' reminded Jeanette.

'All right. We'll eat it and talk things over. You'd better go back to your mother, Jeanette.'

'If you say, *monsieur*.' Jeanette went out.

'Now let's try to fix a definite plan,' went on Ginger. 'What do you suggest?'

'We've got two angles to cover. First, someone ought to follow Algy to Castillon, to make contact with him and let him know what has happened here, and to find out what he knows. Two, someone will have to go to Peille to rescue Henri.'

'That sounds a tall order.'

'We can't just abandon him.'

'No, by Jove, that's right enough,' agreed Bertie.

'I'll tell you what,' suggested Ginger. 'You push off right away to Castillon and try to get hold of Algy—assuming he's there. Tell him about Henri, and say I've gone to Peille in the hope of getting him out. When I've got him I'll join you at Castillon. If for any reason you have to leave the place, come back to the Quai de Plaisance. We'd better keep that the permanent rendezvous.'

'That's all right, but do you think you can manage to get to Peille?'

'I'm jolly well going to try it. After all, Henri is Jeanette's brother.'

Bertie finished his soup and put his eyeglass in his pocket. 'And you're the bold Sir Galahad? Well, don't let this damsel-in-distress stuff—'

'What are you talking about?' broke in Ginger angrily. 'I should have gone after Henri, anyway.'

'Of course—of course—absolutely, old boy.' Bertie rose and picked up his guitar. 'Well, if you're satisfied with the arrangement I'll toddle along and visit the cats of Castillon. I'll give you one tip. You can trust François Budette. If things get really hot, go to him for advice. Tell him who you are, and all that sort of thing. If for any reason I don't show up again, go to him. At a pinch I may be able to get a message through to him.'

'Good enough,' agreed Ginger.

Bertie put what was left of the bread in his pocket and went to the door. 'Don't let those dark eyes of young Jeanette take you too far off your course—if you get my meaning,' he advised.

'You go to—Castillon,' snarled Ginger.

Bertie chuckled and departed on his mission.

As soon as he had gone Ginger got out of bed and started to dress. His leg was stiff, and he had a moment of giddiness that made him clutch the bedpost; but the spasm soon passed, and apart from a feeling of lassitude, which he put down to loss of blood, he felt fairly normal. When Jeanette came up a few minutes later to collect the dishes she found him fully dressed.

She uttered a cry of surprise. 'Why this you do, *monsieur*?' she scolded.

'Because *mademoiselle*, I have work to do,' answered Ginger.

'But where are you going?'

'To Peille, to see Henri. We can't leave him there. Once the police get him to Nice it will be more difficult to save him. I am going at once, hoping to be in Peille before he leaves.'

'But where is Monsieur Bertie?'

'He has other work to do, in Castillon.'

'But you cannot do this, *monsieur*,' protested Jeanette.

'Why not?'

'Because, in the first place, you are wounded, and it is many kilometres to Peille; and secondly because the police they look for you. You have no chance of getting out of the principality.'

Keen as he was to go, Ginger perceived the truth of these arguments. 'Let us deal with these things one at a time,' he said. 'Is it possible to get a vehicle to take me—at least, up the hill as far as La Turbie?'

'Vehicle? What is this?'

'A taxi.'

'There are no taxis now in Monaco.'

'A horse and cart, then?'

121

'What few horses there are are weak from want of food. They are rarely seen out. By taking one you would draw attention to yourself. It might be possible to get a donkey.'

Ginger blinked. 'A donkey?'

'But yes. Many people here use donkeys to fetch the wood, the coal, to carry the fish and vegetables in the basket. My aunt has such a one.'

'Will she sell it, or hire it to me?'

'I will ask Mama to speak to her about it.'

'Would this donkey carry me, do you think?'

'Surely. The donkey is a good little beast, better than a horse on these mountain roads, which is why we use him. He is used to carrying people. I will ask Mama of this.'

Jeanette called her mother, who came in looking as though she had been crying. The matter was explained to her. The expedition, she opined, was *fantastique*, but she would ask about the donkey.

Ginger pulled out a wad of notes that made her gasp. 'Take as much money as you think will be necessary, *madame*, and say that if the expedition is successful I may be able to bring the donkey back, but this, of course, I cannot promise.'

At first Madame Ducoste refused to take any money, but Ginger pressed some on her and she departed on her errand.

'Now what can I do about myself so that the police will not recognize me?' asked Ginger.

'We must make you into a Monégasque,' declared Jeanette, smiling. 'For clothes there is no trouble, for you may have those of Henri. They are old, but that is all the better. But your face is too white and your

122

hair is too red. For your face I have the very thing—
and perhaps for your hair. Wait.'

Jeanette went out and returned with a bottle and a
small jar. 'These were left here by our last English
lady,' she explained. 'This oil in the bottle is for to
make the skin brown, to prevent the burning when one
bathes in the sun. The visitors here all use it to make
them brown. *Voila! monsieur.*'

'What's that in the jar?'

'Mascara, *monsieur.* Some girls use it to make their
eyebrows black. For me that is not necessary. Perhaps
it will make your hair black. You may try while I fetch
the clothes of Henri.'

With Henri's clothes, the sun-bronze oil, and the
mascara, Ginger so altered his appearance that when
he looked in the mirror it gave him a shock. They were
laughing about it when a clatter of hooves announced
the arrival of *madame* with the donkey. They went down
to the door to see it, and found it already saddled,
with panniers, attached to the saddle, on each side. Its
name, Ginger learned, was Lucille.

'If you are questioned, for what purpose are you
going to Peille?' asked *madame* shrewdly. 'It would be
a good thing to know.'

Ginger hadn't thought of that. 'What can I fetch?'
he asked.

'You could be fetching olive oil or wine from Monsieur Bonafacio, who is a seller of such things in Peille,'
suggested *madame*.

'I'll remember it,' promised Ginger, feeling in his
pockets to make sure that he had transferred everything
from his own clothes.

Madame went through to the kitchen and returned

with a parcel which she thrust in one of the panniers. 'You will need food,' she explained.

Ginger took the bridle and held out his hands. '*Au revoir, madame*,' he said with sincerity. 'I shall always remember your kindness.'

'*Adieu, monsieur*. Give my love to Henri if you see him.'

Ginger turned to Jeanette and took her hands. '*Au revoir*, Jeanette,' he said softly.

'You will come back, *monsieur*?' she whispered.

'Not all the Axis* armies shall keep me from you,' swore Ginger, and moved by an impulse he kissed her on the forehead.

Jeanette broke away and ran into the house.

Ginger turned to her mother. 'Have I done wrong?' he asked in a hurt voice.

Madame smiled a knowing smile. 'I ran away from my husband just so,' she answered. 'Women are like that,' she added vaguely. 'I'll take care of her. Go with God, *monsieur*. We shall pray for you.'

Ginger raised his faded beret. 'Thank you, *madame*. *Au revoir*.'

He turned to the donkey, who was watching these proceedings with big brown eyes. 'Come on, Lucille,' he said. 'Let's go.'

Holding the reins, followed by Lucille, he set off down the narrow street.

* The armies of Germany and Italy.

Chapter 11
The Cats of Castillon

Still hoping to see the girl in the blue shawl, Algy hastened up the hill to Monte Carlo, looked along the seats of the famous terraces in front of the casino, and walked through the spacious gardens to the main road that runs behind them, the road that runs through Mentone to the Italian frontier, only a few miles distant. Observing an open market on the left he turned into it, still seeking the girl in blue. There were many coloured shawls, but none of the particular tint he hoped to see. Several loungers were leaning against some iron railings, watching the scene, and he addressed them.

'*Bon jour messieurs*. What would be my best way of getting to Castillon?'

'To Castillon!' cried two of the men together.

'Yes.'

One of the men, looking at the sky as though invoking inspiration, exclaimed, 'Now, why would a man go to Castillon?'

Algy moved uncomfortably. He had a feeling he was on dangerous ground. 'It is just an excursion, to look round the place,' he said casually, trying to pass the matter off as of no importance.

'An excursion! Ah, well—that's different,' said another man, a swarthy Monégasque. 'Nobody goes to Castillon, but if you take the autobus to Mentone, there is, I hear, a bus service once a day, some time in the afternoon, to Sospel, and the road passes at no great distance from Castillon. Doubtless the driver would put you off there if you asked him.'

'*Merci*. And where do I catch the bus for Mentone?'

The man pointed to the steps of a church. 'The bus leaves there at ten o'clock.'

Algy thanked the speaker, and glancing at the church clock, saw that he had more than an hour to wait, so he joined a noisy throng in a nearby café and made a breakfast of bread and imitation coffee. Just before ten, seeing people beginning to collect at the bus stop, he went over and took his place.

He found himself standing next to a dark, fierce-looking man, dressed in black, carrying a heavy shopping bag. To pass the time, and perhaps learn something of interest, he attempted to get into conversation with him, but received a rebuff so different from the usual courteous manner of the people that he was astonished. He said no more. The bus came in nearly an hour late, a circumstance that appeared to occasion no surprise among those who waited for it. There was a rush that packed it to suffocation, after which, with a crash of gears, the driver set off at a pace that made Algy close his eyes, although the other passengers continued to talk as though nothing unusual was happening.

Ten minutes later, in an avenue backed by tall white villas, evidently the outskirts of an important town, the bus was stopped by two Italian police. It was a bad moment for Algy, who thought they might be looking for him. But this proved not to be the case. The police merely made the driver pull into a private drive, and informed him, and the passengers, that the vehicle would be going no farther. They were advised to walk.

126

No explanation was given. Algy got out with the others and walked the rest of the way into Mentone.

He became aware that a curious sort of excitement was in the air. Italian and French police were everywhere. People stood on their doorsteps, or looked down through their windows. Those in the streets formed in little groups, but when a group grew to more than half a dozen people it was broken up by police. Algy spoke to several people, but nobody seemed to know what was happening – or else they were disinclined to comment. With some difficulty he made his way to the market in the centre of the town, from where, he was informed, the Sospel bus usually departed. He noticed, without any real interest, that the swarthy bad-tempered man whom he had seen in Monaco, and later in the bus, had dropped his shopping bag against the kerb, and was also waiting, presumably, for the same bus. It was now nearly noon.

Algy made further inquiries about the Sospel bus, but the answers he received confused rather than helped him. Some people said it would go at two o'clock. Others said three. Others said it would not go at all. Contemplating walking, he asked how far it was to Castillon, but the inquiry was met with such curious expressions that he gave it up. One man said it was eight kilometres; another said it was twenty, and uphill all the way. Algy came to the conclusion that they were all mad, in which he did them an injustice; for the fact is, in a straight line, as an aeroplane might fly, it is but five miles from Mentone to Castillon; but as the road zig-zags through the mountains the distance is ten miles.

To pass the time he sat at one of the outside tables of a café from which he would be able to watch the bus stop, and made a fair meal of vegetable soup and fish. While he was sitting there a lorry filled with Italian troops roared through. Others followed. Then came tanks and armoured cars. Algy could not make out what was happening.

A radio loud-speaker presently solved the problem for him. In an official announcement the speaker informed the people that British and American troops had invaded Algeria and Morocco, and as a result the whole of France was being occupied by German and Italian troops.

This news shook Algy not a little, but as far as he could see it made little difference to his own private expedition, except that there would now be more enemy troops about, and the Italian police would no doubt tighten their grip on the civilian population.

It was after four when the Sospel bus, its radiator spurting steam, drew in. Algy got a seat, but gave it up to an old woman with a basket of vegetables. He found himself standing next to the swarthy man whom he had seen in Monaco, and concluded that fate had decided to throw them together. Thinking perhaps the hardships of travelling had taken the edge off the man's ill humour, he tried his luck again with a question.

'Is it possible that this bus will ever reach Sospel?' he asked, smiling.

The man's eyes stared into his own from a distance of about a foot, so closely were they pressed in the overloaded vehicle.

'I do not care whether it gets to Sospel or not,' was the curt reply.

'Ah! Perhaps you are only going as far as Castillon?' suggested Algy hopefully, and was instantly appalled by the expression of hate and fear that leapt into the dark eyes. 'What's the matter?' he went on. 'Is some-body treading on your foot?'

There was no answer.

'You'll have more room when I get out, for I'm only going as far as Castillon,' went on Algy cheerfully. 'How far is it?' he added.

The man almost hissed in his face. 'I've never heard of the place.'

'Oh,' said Algy. 'I was hoping that you would be able to tell me where to get off.'

After that he gave it up, and for nearly an hour he clung to a metal bar as the bus puffed and snorted, with innumerable stops, up a hill that seemed inter-minable. It panted and lurched round bends, some of them so sharp that the driver had to 'tack' round them, with a wall of rock on one side and a sheer drop on the other.

The driver stopped at a village. Several people got out, making a little more room, for which Algy was thankful. The swarthy man found a seat. The bus went on again. But it did not get far. One or two lorries filled with Italian soldiers had already come down the hill, and now the bus was stopped by a squad of troops. Everyone was ordered to dismount. The road was closed, it was announced. It was wanted by the military.

Algy spoke to a tired-looking workman. 'Are we near the Italian frontier?' he asked.

The man pointed to the mountains on the other side of the chasm which the bus had followed. 'That,' he said, 'is Italy.'

Algy began to understand why the Italian troops were so thick. 'How far is it up the road to Castillon?' he asked.

The man started. 'To Castillon? Why would you want to go there?'

Algy smiled sheepishly, wondering what was the matter with the place that the name should have such a curious effect on people. 'I just wanted to have a look round,' he explained.

'Oh, that,' was the answer. 'It is, perhaps, an hour's walk—that is, if you care to face the rocks when you see the village on your left, across the *col*. If you keep to the road it will take you longer.'

After thanking the man for what sounded like reliable information, Algy walked on up the hill, away from the stationary bus and the gesticulating crowd around it. Some of the women were furious, demanding bitterly to be told how they were to get their heavy baskets to Sospel. Some sat on their baskets, accepting the situation philosophically. A few had started walking.

It was now about five o'clock, as near as Algy could judge, and the sun was already sinking, far away to the left, towards the gaunt peaks of the maritime alps. Anxious to reach his objective before darkness fell he strode on, and soon outdistanced the other travellers— that is, all except one. Well ahead on the long dusty road he made out a man walking quickly, and recognized his churlish travelling companion. He was not sorry to see the back of him, and when, presently, the man disappeared from sight, he thought no more about him.

It was about three-quarters of an hour later, with dusk closing in, that he caught his first glimpse of what he knew must be his destination—a cluster of grey dwellings, with their feet, it seemed, welded into the rock on which they were built. But between him and the village lay a gorge, and a wilderness of jagged rock

130

which, in the half light, he did not feel like crossing; and when soon afterwards, he came to a footpath branching off the road in the desired direction, he was glad he had not attempted it.

He now found himself in a world of grey rocks, so harsh, so desolate, that he found it hard to believe that he was only a few miles from a fashionable town, with all its modern conveniences. From a distance of perhaps two hundred yards he paused to survey a scene as dreary as nature could devise. On all sides stretched the rock, sometimes falling into chasms, and sometimes rising in gaunt peaks against the sky. Not a soul was in sight, not even near the village, which lay like a pile of grey ashes among limestone. Over everything hung an indefinable atmosphere of desolation and decay, of brooding melancholy, of things long dead.

Suddenly he saw a movement. A man, a man in black, carrying a heavy bag, was just entering the village. He saw him only for a moment, but before he disappeared among the houses he had recognized him. It was his bad-tempered travelling companion. He was, too, it seemed, a liar, thought Algy, for the man had said that he had never heard of Castillon. Yet here he was, just going into the place. Wondering at this strange behaviour Algy walked on.

Keeping to the track he soon came to the first houses, and the village street; and for the first time he began to understand why his references to the place had met with such a strange reception. It was dead. Deserted. Many of the houses were in ruins. Others were crumbling. Doors stood open to the sunset. From one house a shutter hung pathetically on a single hinge. The village, a curious mixture of houses and stables, seemed to have been piled up rather than built. The houses conformed with no pattern. They were all sizes, heights, and widths. All were of the stone on which they were built. Mysterious turnings twisted between them. Sinister steps led down into mouldering vaults and cellars. One door had a slit for letters, as if awaiting the arrival of the postman. Over everything hung the silence of death.

Algy started as something moved near his left shoulder. But it was only a cat, a black, mangy creature, with baleful eyes that watched his every movement. Another cat walked slowly across the track in front of him; once it paused to regard him with a long, penetrating stare. Then it went on and disappeared into one of the cellars.

Algy walked forward a few paces. Everywhere he looked he saw cats, black cats, long, thin, emaciated cats, with red-rimmed eyes. Most of them seemed to be afflicted with a dreadful mange. He understood now what the boatman on the Quai de Plaisance meant about cats. He had never seen so many cats. Everywhere he looked, eyes were turned on him with such suspicion and hate that he felt an uncomfortable chill creep down his spine. Looking about him he walked on, determined to make the most of the few minutes of twilight that remained.

There should, he thought, be at least one occupied house, for to his certain knowledge a man had just arrived. Where had he gone? Why had he been so secretive, so furtive in his movements—or had he caught the habit from the cats? Even then the last thing in his mind was that he had incurred the man's enmity.

He stopped to look into a house, moving a shutter in order to do so. Unexpectedly, the shutter came away in his hand, so that he stumbled, and this may have

132

saved his life; for at that precise moment there was a vicious thud, and looking up to see what had caused it, he saw, still quivering in the windowsill, a knife. Whirling round to discover who had thrown it he was just in time to see the black-coated man disappearing into a narrow side turning.

Algy was after him in a flash. He did not know who the man was, and he bore him no ill will, but he was not prepared to have knives thrown at him—at least, not without knowing what it was all about.

Had the man not stumbled and fallen among the loose rocks it is unlikely that he would have caught him. The fellow was up again in a moment, but the brief delay had been his undoing. Before he could get into his stride Algy was covering him with his automatic. Even so, he was prepared to be reasonable.

'Not so fast, my friend,' he said coldly, speaking in French. 'Why did you throw a knife at me? What have I done to you?'

The man glared. 'Spy!' He fairly spat the word.

'I am not spying on you, anyway,' declared Algy.

'You followed me here.'

'I did not,' denied Algy.

'Then why do you come to Castillon?'

'Why do *you* come here?'

'I have business here.'

'So have I.' An idea suddenly struck Algy. 'Our business may concern the same thing.'

'Doubtless,' was the curt reply.

'Tell me why you came here,' invited Algy.

'I shall tell you nothing.'

Algy tried a shot in the dark. 'Where is the person you came here to see?'

The man started. Then he smiled sardonically, and

an instant later, Algy knew the reason. A voice behind him, a woman's voice, spoke.

'Don't move, or I shall shoot you. Drop that pistol.'

As if to carry conviction something small and hard was pressed between Algy's shoulders. He dropped his pistol. It fell with a harsh clatter on the stones. The man leapt forward and snatched it up.

Turning slowly Algy found himself staring at the girl he had last seen on the Quai de Plaisance—the girl in the blue shawl. But for the first time he could see her clearly. Her face, moulded on classic lines, and very beautiful, was pale. Her head was proudly poised, and dark flashing eyes met his own without a trace of nervousness. A faint smile played about the corners of perfectly formed lips. Her clothes were those of a girl of the country, but her general bearing, which they could not hide, was not. Algy did not know what to make of her.

'Well,' he began, and would have gone on, but she stopped him with a gesture.

'Talking will lead to nothing,' she said coldly.

The man suddenly broke in with a request that the prisoner be shot forthwith, but the girl in blue stopped him with a glance of her flashing eyes. It was obvious to Algy that the man was subordinate to the girl, in whatever business they were engaged.

'He followed me all the way from Monaco,' said the man.

Algy ignored him. To the girl he said, 'I should like to talk to you, *mademoiselle*.'

'It will do no good,' she returned curtly. 'We have been into all the arguments before. Now it is war.' To the man she said, 'Mario, put him in the cellar until it is decided what shall be done with him. You know the

134

one I mean?' And with that she turned on her heel and walked away.

Algy called after her. He wanted to know what she was doing on the Quai de Plaisance, but she walked on without looking back, and the man she called Mario told him to make less noise.

'Walk,' he ordered, 'and do not talk.'

Algy shrugged his shoulders. For the moment, at any rate, there was no alternative than to obey. With his own pistol uncomfortably close to his back he was marched to one of the several cellars, one that had a stout door. He was thrust inside. The door crashed shut behind him, and he was left in darkness.

Chapter 12
Bertie Picks a Lemon

Bertie left Ginger with the fixed plan of getting to Castillon as quickly as possible. He recalled, now, having heard of the place, although he had never had occasion to make a visit. In any case, he had always understood that the place was a ruin.

He felt that he ought to let François know where he was going, and with that object in view he proceeded first to the Condamine. François appeared with an alacrity that suggested he had been on the watch. They held a brief but enlightening conversation. Bertie told François that he was going to Castillon, and that the man who had asked about the place, on the quay, shortly after dawn, was a friend on the same errand as himself. He also told him about Ginger, and said that he proposed, if circumstances made it necessary, to use François' house as a letter-box, an arrangement to which the boatman readily agreed.

'But, milord,' said he, 'you will find it difficult now to get to Castillon.'

'Why?' asked Bertie. 'Speaking from memory, the village lies near the Sospel road.'

To this François assented.

'Does not the autobus still run to Sospel?' inquired Bertie.

'That I do not know,' confessed François, 'but I should doubt it. I comprehend, milord, that you have not heard the news?'

'What news?'

'All the roads near the frontier are to be closed—if they are not already closed.'

'In heavens name, why?'

'During the night the British and the Americans landed in Morocco and Algeria. Now Hitler and Mussolini occupy between them all France. *Regardez!*' François pointed to the main road down which military traffic was streaming.

Bertie was dumbfounded. This development came to him as a complete surprise—as it did to most people.

'This is not going to make things easier, *mon vieux*,' he observed. 'Is the road to Mentone closed?'

'So it is said. And if that road is now closed, surely, too, will be the road to Sospel, which skirts the frontier. They say the roads may be opened later.' François spat, thoughtfully. 'I should say, milord, that for you, this morning, the Sospel road is a thing to avoid.'

'But I must get to Castillon,' declared Bertie. 'How else can I get there? There is no other road.'

'There is no other road, but there are the *chemins muletiers*.'

'Ah! The mule tracks that were used in the old days, before the roads.'

'*Oui*.' François snapped his fingers. '*Bon-ca!*' he ejaculated. 'I have an inspiration. I know a man who every day brings vegetables down from his terraces behind St. Agnes. He takes the back way. Since he deals in food he has been allowed petrol for his *camionette*.* St. Agnes is more than half way to Castillon. There is no road between the two, but there is an old mule path, as there is between all the villages. If my friend will

* French: van

137

take you in his *camionette* to St. Agnes, by marching quickly you would be in Castillon by the setting of the sun.'

'How far is it from St. Agnes to Castillon?'

François shrugged. 'Four hours, perhaps,' he replied, resorting to the usual way of counting distances in mountain country, by time, and not miles.

'Good,' declared Bertie. 'Where is this friend of yours?'

'He should be at the market, in Monte Carlo, if he has not already left for home. Let us go and find out.'

It took them some time to get to the market on account of the traffic, and the crowds that thronged the pavements to watch. And having reached the market they found everything in a state of chaos, customers and stall-holders alike having gone to the steps of the church to watch the procession passing by. People who wanted to leave had also been held up by the invasion of the Italian troops. François found his friend's *camionette*—a battered light lorry, filthy and delapidated beyond description—but it was twelve o'clock before the man himself appeared.

He greeted François warmly and slapped him on the back. 'By God! These are times,' he cried.

François broached his subject, but did not mention Castillon. He merely said that his friend was anxious to get to St. Agnes.

'I shall be lucky to get there myself,' declared the vendor of vegetables. 'The roads are full of these Italians. Doubtless we shall get to St. Agnes sooner or later, and if your friend cares to come with me he will be welcome, but it would be better, I think, to wait until the road is clearer.'

With this the others were bound to agree, so they adjourned to a café for lunch.

It was two o'clock before the *camioneur** suddenly declared his intention of going home, which suited Bertie, who was finding the delay irritating. He said good-bye to François and promised to look him up when he returned.

The first part of the journey was slow, for there was still a lot of traffic about, but once off the main road the driver whirled his vehicle up the formidable corniche road that led to St. Agnes with a confidence born of familiarity. Accustomed though he was to the mountain roads, Bertie covered his face at many of the hairpin bends where the road hangs like a ledge over a drop of a thousand feet or more; and he was weak at the knees when the vehicle finally skidded to a standstill in the village, which is not really a village so much as a cluster of old houses clinging precariously to a spire of rock, as bare as a boulder, over two thousand feet high. Why anyone should choose to live in such a place is one of the great mysteries that have never been solved—unless it is to sit in wonder at the marvellous panorama of sea and coast spread out below.

'By the way,' said Bertie to his driver as they dismounted, 'where is Castillon?'

'*Voila*!' answered the man, pointing. 'There it is.'

Following the direction with his eyes Bertie saw a village similar to the one in which he was standing about three miles distant. It looked so near that it seemed incredible that it would take four hours to cover the space between them—until he looked at the chaos

---

* French: van driver

of ridges and ravines that intervened. He saw that he would be lucky to reach his objective before nightfall.

He pointed to a track which dived down the mountain on the landward side. 'That, I suppose, is the track to Castillon?' he observed.

'It is,' answered the driver. 'Only no one uses it.'

Bertie thanked him for the lift, waited for him to go, and then, glancing round to make sure that he was unobserved, set off on his long hike. An hour later, from the crest of a ridge, Castillon looked just as far away, so he increased his pace. All around the country lay silent and deserted, which was not to be wondered at, for except for a few artificial terraces to which clung olives and sad-looking cypress trees, there was nothing but grey, sun-bleached limestone.

The sun was fast dropping into the mountains when he came within striking distance of his objective. He sat down to rest for a few minutes. Fit as he was, the muscles of his calves ached unmercifully, as is usually the case when a man accustomed to walking on pavements finds himself in mountain country. He lit one of the few cigarettes that remained in his case; and as he smoked he looked at the sad grey ruins before him, slightly below, and perhaps two hundred and fifty yards away.

Suddenly he stiffened. Jeanette had distinctly said that the village was abandoned, yet he was sure that he had seen somebody move, somebody in blue. He continued to watch. The speck of blue appeared again from behind some houses, and he saw it was a girl, with a blue shawl draped round her shoulders. She halted by a rock, as if waiting. It looked as if Jeanette had been right about a girl in blue writing on the wall. A girl in a blue shawl had written the word Castillon

140

on the wall of the Quai de Plaisance, and now, here was a girl, thus dressed, in the village. That could hardly be coincidence, thought Bertie. His weariness forgotten, he was about to hurry forward when he saw another movement. This time it was a man in black. He was walking quickly towards the spot where the girl was waiting, as if keeping an appointment.

Bertie continued to watch. Could it be possible, he wondered, that in some way these people, these strange events, were associated with Biggles? It seemed impossible, and yet . . . there was the blue writing on the wall. Surely there must be some connection?

The man reached the point where the girl was standing. They met. For a minute they stood together as if talking; then they disappeared into a narrow lane, behind houses which hid them from view. Hardly had they disappeared when, to Bertie's astonishment, a third figure appeared. He recognized Algy. He was approaching the village from the opposite direction, having arrived, it seemed, from the Sospel road. He was walking in the tracks of the man in black.

In his excitement Bertie nearly shouted a greeting, but remembering that there were other people about, he thought better of it. Instead, he hurried forward.

Half-way to the village there was a dip in the ground that hid it from view, and when he reached the far side Algy was nowhere in sight. He watched for a minute or two, hoping to see him among the houses, but when he did not appear he continued on his way. Once he thought he heard voices, raised as if in anger, but he was not sure. He went nearer, and at last, having reached the outskirts, he paused to survey it from the cover of a gnarled lemon tree, on which hung some half-ripe fruit. Nothing happened. Thinking it might assuage his thirst, he casually picked a lemon and went on.

Turning a corner, he came suddenly face to face with the black-coated man. It was not the actual meeting, nor was it the black coat that brought an exclamation of incredulity to his lips. It was the face of the man who wore it. For he was the very last person he expected to see there. It was Mario, the waiter of the Chez Rossi, the man who, the previous night, had struck him on the head and then thrown him down the Escalier Ste. Dévote.

Fortunately for Bertie the waiter appeared to be equally astonished, with the result that for five breathless seconds they simply stood and stared at each other. Bertie spoke first.

'By Jove!' he said, 'you're the blighter who dotted me on the skull last night!'

Mario did not answer. His hand flashed to his belt, and came up holding a slim-bladed stiletto. With a snort of anger Bertie used the weapon that came readiest to his hand. In fact, it was already in his hand. He flung the lemon—and he flung it hard. It hit the Italian in the eye and brought from him a cry of pain. Bertie followed the fruit, and dodging the waving stiletto, hit the waiter in the stomach. 'I'll teach you, you nasty feller,' he said. The waiter went over backwards among the rocks, falling with some force. Apparently he knocked his knuckles, for the stiletto flew out of his hand. Bertie picked it up and tossed it away.

Feeling that he had done enough he took a pace backward, prepared to open negotiations. But this did not suit the waiter, who, with a snarl of fury, charged, head down, like a horned animal. Impeded by his guitar, Bertie could not avoid the rush, so they grappled in a clinch, the man still snarling, using teeth and nails, Bertie silent, trying to break away to use his fists. Mario kicked Bertie on the skin, and the pain moved him to wrath.

'All right, my garlic-eating dish-wiper; two can play at that game,' he rasped, and stamped on the man's foot. With a howl of agony Mario released his hold, whereupon Bertie got in a hook to the jaw that stretched him on his back for the count.

Slightly winded, Bertie sat down to recover his breath and his composure. He took out his monocle, polished it, and putting it in his eye, regarded his antagonist with disfavour. He lit a cigarette and waited for him to recover, for there were several questions he was anxious to ask—among other things, why he had killed Zabani, why he had hidden the Pernod show-card and why he had tried to murder him. Then he remembered that Algy was somewhere in the village, so he struck a few chords on his guitar to let him know that he was there. Algy did not come. Instead, Mario sat up, holding his jaw, eyeing his victor malevolently.

'Now, before you play any more tricks, my merry dart-thrower, just you listen to me,' said Bertie severely. 'I'm going to ask you some questions, and if you don't answer them I shall hand you over to the police for letting the daylight into Signor Zabani. Oh, yes, I know all about that.'

Mario started, half closing his eyes. 'You are not of the police?'

'Me? Ha, ha! That's a good one. No, I am not of the police—not the French, the Italian or the Monégasque. Why did you knife Zabani?'

'If you must know, it was by order of the Camorra.

143

I am a Camorrista. Take care, or you will have a knife in, you, too.'

'And Zabani? He upset the chief Camorrista—is that it?'

'Yes. Take care you do not upset him. Why have you come here?'

Bertie smiled faintly. 'If I told you, my little soup-ladler, you would not believe me.'

'Tell me why you come here and perhaps I can help you,' suggested Mario slyly—and, Bertie thought, unexpectedly.

He drew his fingers across the strings of his guitar. 'I am a troubadour—a troubadour who would sing to a princess.'

Mario's sallow face turned ashen. His eyes seemed to start out from his face. 'You seek—a—princess?' he gasped.

'That's what I said.'

'Do you expect to find one in a place like this?'

Bertie shrugged. 'Who knows? After all, you are at Castillon, and I didn't expect to find you here.'

'What has that to do with the princess?'

'You killed a man who betrayed a princess, *amico*, so would it be so strange if you knew her?'

'So,' breathed Mario, 'that is why you came? To find a princess.'

'That is one reason. Can you help me?'

'Yes,' snapped Mario viciously. 'I can show you one.'

'Now you're talking,' declared Bertie. 'Where is she?'

'Look behind you.'

Half expecting a trick, Bertie glanced behind him and then sprang to his feet in comical surprise. For there, standing within a few paces of him, silhouetted against the sunset, covering him with an automatic,

144

was the girl in the blue shawl. Feeling rather foolish, he raised his hat.

'*Bon soir*,' he stammered. Then he added, taking her to be Italian, 'Or should I say *buona sera**?'

The girl answered in French, with a slight Italian accent. 'Did I hear you say you came here to find a princess?'

'That is correct,' Bertie assured her.

'Why?'

'Because only a princess can tell me what has become of my best friend.'

'You are English, I think?'

'Very, very English,' answered Bertie.

'Ah.' The girl drew a deep breath that might have been relief. 'Do you know the name of this princess?'

'No.'

'Was it the Principessa Marietta Loretto de Palma?'

Bertie stared. He was finding it hard to keep pace with the conversation. 'It might have been,' he acknowledged. 'Do you know this lady?'

The girl in blue smiled faintly. '*Monsieur*, she stands before you.'

'By Jove! Really?' Remembering himself, Bertie bowed. He indicated the waiter. 'And this man?'

'Mario is my faithful servant,' answered the princess quietly. 'His father and his father before him served my family.'

'I see,' murmured Bertie. 'I think I begin to understand.'

The princess turned to Mario. 'You did not tell me that you had killed Zabani?' she said in a voice as brittle as ice.

* Italian: Good evening

145

Mario looked disconsolate. 'Your pardon, highness. But the order came from—higher up.'

'The jolly old chief Camorrista—what?' put in Bertie.

The princess turned on him in a flash. 'Silence!' she said curtly. To Mario she said, 'You can explain this to me later. Turning back to Bertie, she went on, 'Have you by any chance a friend who might have come to Castillon this afternoon?'

'Why—er—yes, by jingo!' replied Bertie. 'In fact, I know he's here. I saw him arrive a few minutes ago.'

'Was he also looking for a princess?'

'Absolutely—yes, absolutely.'

The princess turned to Mario. 'Release him,' she ordered. Then, to Bertie, 'and now you have found the princess—what then?'

'I should like to see her kitchen—I believe it is a *bon cuisine*,' answered Bertie meaningly. And as he spoke, with his toe, he carelessly traced a triangle in a patch of dust.

The princess smiled. 'Follow me, sir,' she said quietly.

Chapter 13
Pilgrimage to Peille

After one glance at the steep slopes behind Monte Carlo, Ginger decided that the only way to get to La Turbie, as the first stage in his journey to Peille, was by road. This involved a risk of being stopped and questioned, but it could not be avoided. He was in no condition for rock climbing. At the bottom of the hill he mounted his animal, and setting its face to the gradient, allowed it to choose its own gait.

His fears about being stopped were well founded, for he was stopped twice, once at the frontier of Monaco and France by two Monégasque soldiers, and later by two Italians, but evidently he looked the part he was playing, for they treated him as a joke and allowed him to pass without asking embarrassing questions. The ascent to the top of the hill occupied two hours.

Once on the lonely road that winds from La Turbie to Peille the way lay clear before him, and he began to enjoy the trip. The sun shone down from a sky of deepest azure. Behind lay the blue Mediterranean, sparkling in the clear air, fringing the distant capes with foam. On the left was the broad fertile valley into which they had jumped on the night of their arrival, its far slopes shining grey with olive groves. Here and there a cypress thrust its spire-like point into the air. On the right the ground rose steeply to the dominant peak of Mont Agel, capped by the fort which its engineers had intended should protect the country against

Italian invaders. Ahead, the road twisted like a grey ribbon through the mountains, not over them, but in the side of the rock, so that it maintained the same level throughout, sometimes curling back upon itself in a sweeping curve to avoid a chasm. From every cranny sprang wild lavender, rosemary and thyme, or sometimes a clump of vicious-looking cactus.

Just beyond half-way the scene began to change. It became more harsh. A solitary eagle appeared, gliding high on rigid pinions. On the right the rocks rose pinnacle on pinnacle to towering peaks. To the left the land was a chaos of beetling crags and sheer precipices, along the edge of which the road now ran a precarious course. At one point, marked significantly with a shrine, a track wound dizzily into the mountains; a lolling signpost announced that it was a *route strategical* to St. Agnes.

Ginger went on, overawed by the immensity of the landscape. The chasm on the left became a yawning gorge so deep that the bottom was lost in purple shadows. The road crumbled along the edge of it without any kind of protection to prevent a careless traveller from falling headlong into the void. The donkey, wise like all its race, kept well away from the brink. At one place the beetling crags on the right overhung the road, so that it looked like a tunnel with one side torn away. The donkey's little hooves rang with a hollow sound.

Not a single traveller did Ginger meet. The sun rose high into the heavens, flamed across its zenith, and began to fall towards the west; and still the land lay grey and lifeless. Of Peille there was no sign, and as the day wore on he began to wonder if he was on the right road. Soon afterwards, rounding a formidable buttress, he saw the village before him, a huddle of houses crouching on a lip of rock that hung like a shelf over the edge of the world. Far below a blue thread marked the course of a river. On its bank was another village into which, from his dizzy height, Ginger could have dropped a stone.

A small boy, in rags, barefoot, came up the road to meet him, strolling carelessly along the edge of the chasm. '*Bon jour, monsieur*,' he greeted.

Ginger pointed to the village ahead. 'Have I arrived at Peille?'

'*Oui, monsieur*.'

Ginger pointed down at the village far below. 'And that one?'

'La Grave de Peille.'

'Thank you, my little one,' answered Ginger. 'Here's a *sou* for you.'

The lad caught the coin adroitly, and dashed back to the village with his prize.

Ginger shouted after him, 'Where is the sanitorium?'

The boy pointed to a large oblong building on the right of the road, standing a little way back, at the entrance to the village. 'There it is,' he called.

'Thank you,' replied Ginger. He tightened his reins. 'Whoa, Lucille. This is where we must stop to think.'

He had no clear idea of what he was going to do, having purposely deferred thinking about it until he had made a reconnaissance of the sanitorium. And now he was in sight of it there was little to see. The hospital was a large, perfectly plain white building, standing alone on a slight eminence on the right of the road. It was about a hundred yards from the village, on the side nearest to him. The front door and all the windows stood wide open, although some were shaded by blinds. There was a long line of outbuildings slightly to the

149

rear. Between these buildings and the main structure two rows of laundry—pyjamas, nightshirts, towels and blue linen overalls—hung limply in the sun. Behind, a grey limestone bank rose steeply for several hundred feet to end in a jagged ridge. Into the *massif**, not far from where Ginger stood surveying the scene, a ravine wound a curving course upwards, providing foothold for a number of olive trees. Not a soul was in sight. Nothing moved—not even the washing on the line.

There appeared to be little point in watching this uninspiring spectacle, so Ginger decided first to tether the patient Lucille, and then, by direct inquiry, ascertain if Henri was still there. In this he was encouraged by the apparent absence of police and soldiers.

He led Lucille a little way into the ravine and tethered her in the restful shade of the olives, allowing her enough rope to browse on the rough herbiage. This done he walked diagonally across the road to the front entrance of the sanitorium. Reaching it, he saw beyond the open door a large cool hall. There was no one in it. The only furniture was a form and one or two chairs against the walls, and a coat and hat rack on which hung several white jackets and other garments, presumably the property of the staff. All this was quite usual for a French country hospital.

Ginger rang the bell. After a brief delay an old grey-bearded man came slowly, yawning, out of a side room, where apparently he had been resting. His jacket was unfastened, as was the collar of his shirt. Spectacles were balanced on his nose. On slippered feet he shuffled to where Ginger was waiting.

---

* Group of high mountains

'Pardon, *monsieur*, but are you the janitor?' asked Ginger.

'Yes. What do you want at this time of day? Is a man to have no rest?'

'Having business this way, I have called to make inquiries on behalf of Madame Ducoste,' said Ginger. 'She has been informed that her son Henri is here.'

The janitor came nearer. 'Yes, there is a patient here of that name,' he admitted. 'Who are you? You speak with a queer accent.'

'I am a friend of the family, *monsieur*. I have been away for some years, in Spain.'

'Ah!'

'How is Monsieur Ducoste to-day?'

'Better. They are coming to fetch him away.'

'So we heard. Can I see him?'

'No.'

'But why not? I may never have another opportunity.'

'Because, my young friend, he is in the charge of the police.'

'Yes, we heard that too,' answered Ginger in a melancholy voice. 'Is he in a public ward?'

'No, in a private room.'

Ginger nodded. This was useful information. 'Perhaps the police will let me see him?'

'I doubt it.'

'I can but ask. Where can I find them?'

The janitor yawned. 'The sergeant is not yet back from his siesta. Monsieur André, the *gendarme* of Peille, guards the prisoner in his absence. If you are going to do anything you had better be quick. Ducoste is being taken to Nice. I expect the van here at any moment.'

Ginger caught his breath. 'Where can I find the sergeant?'

'I wouldn't disturb him.'

'Then, with your permission, I will see Monsieur André.'

'No, I can't let you do that, but I will tell him you are here. There is a chance that he may let you see the unfortunate Ducoste, but by order of the prefect all visitors are forbidden.'

'You speak as though you are sorry for Ducoste, *monsieur?*' Ginger spoke as meaningfully as he dared.

The Frenchman threw him a curious glance. 'He would be a brave man, or a foolish one, to say what he thinks, in this country, to-day.'

'Well, will you go and ask Monsieur André if I can see Henri just for a minute?'

'Wait.' The janitor walked off along the main corridor.

Ginger watched him, for he realised that here was an opportunity for discovering where Henri was confined. To his great satisfaction the janitor did not turn up the stairs, but went along to the end door on the right hand side of the corridor. From this Ginger gathered Henri was on the ground floor.

The janitor was absent for about a minute, and then came back. 'No use,' said he. 'Ducoste is not allowed visitors. Police orders.'

'Then I have wasted my time,' muttered Ginger gloomily.

The janitor did not answer at once. He was looking past Ginger's shoulder along the winding road to La Turbie. 'This looks like the police van coming now,' he observed.

Turning, Ginger saw a dark-coloured van creeping

round the lip of the gorge. He had no doubt that the janitor was right, and his heart sank, for although his brain was racing he could not think of a plan that promised the slightest chance of success.

'You'd better be getting along,' advised the janitor.

'Yes, I suppose so,' agreed Ginger disconsolately. But he did not move. He was not yet ready to abandon hope.

As the van drew near the janitor walked forward to the top of the steps, and as it stopped on the road, about twenty paces distant, he went forward to meet the occupants who now emerged. There were three men, not counting the chauffeur. The first was a short, thick-set man in a dark suit. He carried a pair of handcuffs in his left hand. Of the two with him, one was a policeman; the other wore the uniform of the Italian medical service. Talking quietly they moved forward together towards the steps of the sanitorium. The chauffeur lit a cigarette and followed leisurely.

Ginger saw that if he was going to attempt a rescue he had about one minute in which to accomplish it. Once Henri was handcuffed, and in the car, there would be no hope at all, and the realisation of it made him desperate.

The janitor, who had evidently forgotten him, had gone on down the steps and was talking to the newcomers. The whole group halted to hear what he had to say.

If Ginger actually thought he was unaware of it. He acted on impulse. Crossing swiftly to the hat rack he unhooked a white jacket and then sped on down the corridor, putting on the jacket as he went. At the end door he stopped and knocked sharply. A voice invited him to enter. He went in, to find himself in a small

153

whitewashed cubicle. There was an iron bed, and on it a man, his head swathed in bandages. Ginger barely glanced at him. He was looking at a French *gendarme* who, with his tunic unbuttoned, lolled, somewhat uncomfortably, in a wooden chair. To this man Ginger addressed himself.

'We have arrived to take the prisoner to Nice,' he said crisply.

'I thought I heard the car pull up,' announced the *gendarme*, rising.

'The doctor is in the hall—he wants to see you,' went on Ginger, trying to keep his voice natural. 'I'll take charge of the prisoner while you have gone.'

The *gendarme* obeyed the order without the slightest hesitation. To all appearance it did not occur to him to question it. Buttoning his tunic he went out.

The moment the door was closed behind him Ginger locked it on the inside and then went straight to the open window. As he had supposed, the room was at the end of the building, and did not overlook the front, but the side. A short distance away the lines of washing still hung limply in the stagnant air. Just beyond was the ravine in which Lucille rested in the shade. Satisfied with his inspection Ginger turned to Henri and spoke to him tensely.

'We've got about thirty seconds,' he said. 'Are you able to walk?'

Henri, who had been staring hard at Ginger, gave a gasp as he recognised his voice. '*Mon Dieu!* What have you done to yourself? Yes, I'm not as bad as they think.'

'Good. Listen. Get cracking. Get out of the window. Go to the ravine. You'll find a donkey there. Make for Castillon. Wait there.'

154

'But I have no clothes—they have taken them!' cried Henri.

'Then go in your pyjamas—no, there is washing on the line, grab a suit of overalls as you go past. Take your slippers, you will need them. Hurry.'

Henri hastened to the window. Over his shoulder he said, 'What about you?'

'Never mind me. I'll join you at Castillon. I'm going to take the police off your trail to give you a start.'

By this time the handle of the door was being rattled with violence. Henri climbed through the window and disappeared from sight.

To those in the corridor Ginger shouted, 'Just a minute, the door won't open.' Which was perfectly true. It would not open because it was locked. Then he climbed out of the window and ran round to the front of the building.

As he reckoned, the police van was still there, standing where it had been stopped. No one was with it. He sprinted across the front of the hospital and jumped into the driving seat. From the time he had gone down the corridor to Henri's room not more than two minutes had elapsed, and so far everything had worked with the precision of a well-oiled sewing machine. Would the luck hold? It would not, thought Ginger. Nor did it. As he started the engine a shout warned him that he had been seen. The chauffeur came leaping down the steps. But the car was moving now. There was no time to turn, so treading on the accelerator Ginger went straight on. Direction was of no consequence.

There was a fusillade of shots. Two or three bullets hit the van, but without effect. It raced on into the village. The village street, like most streets in the South of France built narrow to give shade during the heat of the day, was only just wide enough to take it. Cats, dogs and chickens, looking up to see death bearing down on them, leapt for their lives as the vehicle shot through, honking to clear the way.

At the far end the road forked. The right fork went up; the left, down. Concerned only with speed Ginger took the one that went down. There was a signpost. As he flashed past it he read, *La Grave de Peille*, but even then he did not fully comprehend what this meant. It was only when he rounded a bend and saw the road plunging down the face of the precipice in a series of incredible zigzags that he remembered the village at the bottom of the gorge. He took his foot off the accelerator and stood on the brakes until they screamed, and filled the car with the stench of burning rubber. But it did not stop. Ginger held his breath. A hairpin bend rushed to meet him. With his eyes starting from his head he spun the wheel. The car dry-skidded round the edge of the gorge with perhaps two inches to spare. Before he could straighten out he was on another bend. This time there was no hope of getting round, for only those who are born to such roads know how to take them at speed.

Ginger spun the wheel desperately. The car skidded, tearing up a cloud of dust, towards the brink, and the frightful void beyond. Ginger knew that it was going over; that nothing could save it; so he did the only thing left to do. He flung himself clear out of the opposite side. His hands closed over the gnarled root of an olive and he hung on for dear life. The van, after hanging at a ghastly angle for a moment, toppled over the edge and disappeared from sight. For a few seconds there was silence; then came such a crashing and banging that seemed as if the whole cliff had collapsed.

Gasping, brushing sweat out of his eyes, Ginger walked to the spot where the car had disappeared, and looking down saw the remains of it, in a cloud of boulders, dust and broken branches, well on its way to the village at the bottom of the chasm.

He staggered back to the olive tree, and for a moment stood there, panting, weak at the knees, completely unnerved by the narrowness of his escape. He looked at his hands curiously, as though they did not belong to him, and saw that they were trembling violently. One had been cut, and was bleeding, but it didn't hurt.

He was still standing there, trying to bring his heart and jarred nerves back to normal, when a shout above reminded him that he was only a short distance from the village, although overhanging trees prevented him from being seen. Obviously, it was no use going back up the road, for he would be certain to meet the police coming down. If he went down, he would be equally certain to find a crowd waiting at the bottom, brought out from the village by the crashing car. Yet if only he could get back to the top road, beyond the sanitorium, he might be able to overtake Henri. He could see parts of the road far above him—or rather, the scar it made round the cliff. The bank between was steep, but not sheer. Stunted olives and fig trees, with their roots well down in the rocks, offered secure handholds.

One thing, he saw, was in his favour. His pursuers would not look up for him; they would look down, assuming that he had gone over with the car. Even if his body were not found it might be supposed that he lay buried under the debris that the car had taken down with it. The police would also suppose that Henri's body lay somewhere down in the valley—at least, he hoped so. They would make a search, and this should give them both a fair start. Drawing a deep breath he began to climb.

The distance to the road, as a bird might fly, was not more than two hundred yards, but as Ginger was compelled to travel it was nearer half a mile. In the van he had come down in perhaps ten seconds, but it was clear that the return journey would take longer—an hour of tortuous, heart-bursting effort. It was dark long before he got to the top, and this did not make his task any easier. Once, from a dizzy perch, he could see the police far below him, running down the dreadful road to La Grave.

When he reached his immediate objective, the village, which lay a short distance to the left, had settled down. He could hear nothing except the distant murmur of voices. With Indian-like stealth he crossed the road, and soon gained the ravine with its group of olives where he had left Lucille. The animal had gone, from which it was reasonably certain Henri had succeeded in getting clear. The thing was to overtake him, to compare notes, and find out how he was standing the journey—a stiff one for an invalid—to Castillon.

Ginger went on through a lonely world of rocks and stunted trees. During his mad escapade he had completely forgotten his wounded leg, but now that the excitement had died down it was beginning to throb. After stopping to loosen the bandages, which gave him some relief, he went on. He went on for perhaps half an hour, by which time he was on top of an enormous saddle-back that commanded a view of the mountains around him. It was like being astride the ridge of the world.

A low whistle made him pull up abruptly, staring among the boulders from which the sound had come.

'Ginger! Is zat you?' said a voice—Henri's voice.

'Yes, it's me,' answered Ginger. 'Have you only got as far as this?'

'Far enough, for the time,' replied Henri, coming forward, leading the donkey.

'Why didn't you go on?'

'I wait for you.'

'But how did you know that I should come this way?'

'From the bank I see what happens,' explained Henri. 'I see you take the car. Name of a dog! It was *superbe*. Then, *zut-alors!* I see you take the road to La Grave. It is suicide. I say to myself it is good-bye. But no. I pray hard. I see you make the quick jump, and in the trees hang like a monkey. The car, she goes *zonk!* You do not go down the road. You do not come up the road. How do I know? Because I am high up and see down on all the bends. I say to myself he must come back to the top road through the trees, to go to Castillon. So I wait. That is all. *Tout simplement**. My friend, you have nerves the most audacious. I am a prisoner. In one minute you make me escape. *Du courage! Magnifique**!* A thousand thanks, *mon ami*. I shall not forget this, no.'

'Neither shall I,' returned Ginger grimly. 'Now, what about pushing on to Castillon?'

'Why, by all the saints, do we go to Castillon, this place of cats?'

'Because Algy and Bertie should be there.'

'But why?'

'We have found a clue and it led to Castillon. I'll

---

* French: So simple!
** French: Such courage! Magnificent!

tell you about it as we go along. If we can get to the place we shall all be together again.'

'*Entendu**. We stay in France a long time now, I think,' said Henri. 'My engine, she goes conk. The old cow.'

'Never mind about that. The question is, can you make the journey to Castillon?'

'But surely. I have the cuts and the bruises, yes, and the head she opens and shuts, but not so bad as I pretend. I think perhaps if I pretend sick I get chance to escape. But no. What I do not understand is how you know I am at Peille?'

Ginger explained, briefly, the circumstances that had led to his visit to the Rue Marinière, and what had happened there.

Of course, Henri wanted to know all about his mother and sister, and this occupied some minutes while they rested. 'And now we had better get on,' concluded Ginger. 'We must get under cover by dawn, or we may be seen, so get aboard Lucille and lead the way. I should like to know what goes on at Castillon.'

They set off up the narrow path.

* French: Understood

Chapter 14
Au Bon Cuisine

Could Ginger only have known what was going on at Castillon he would have been surprised. Events had probably moved far beyond his imagination.

When Bertie had followed the princess he had done so with a certain amount of trepidation. He had no idea of what was going to happen; he was prepared for anything—except what did happen.

A narrow lane wound a serpentine path between dilapidated houses, over fallen masonry, to the outskirts of the village, where a house, larger than most, overlooked a great gash in the rocks that fell away and away, widening as it fell, until at last it dropped into the distant Mediterranean. The girl who had said she was a princess—Bertie only had her word for it—paid no attention to the view. She opened a door from which all paint had long disappeared, and went down two steps into what had evidently been a semi-basement kitchen of considerable size.

'Enter, *monsieur*,' she invited.

'Ah! The *bon cuisine*,' murmured Bertie.

The princess smiled. 'Had you mentioned at first that you had seen the writing on the wall it would have saved you trouble. Now I think I understand.'

'The writing on the wall was not a thing to talk about,' replied Bertie drily.

'But you came here on account of it?'

'Yes.'

161

'But not really to seek a princess, my noble troubadour?'

'Not entirely,' admitted Bertie. 'I was concerned with a knight who had tried to rescue her from the hands of her enemies.'

The princess laughed quietly. 'Are you by any chance the Honourable Lacey?'

Bertie nearly dropped his guitar in astonishment. 'Here, I say, that's a leading question. No, I am not the Honourable Lacey, but he is not far from here. Mario, I think, has gone to fetch him. Ah – here he is.'

Algy, looking slightly bewildered, came down into the kitchen closely followed by Mario. 'Bertie!' he cried, 'are you in the party, too? How did you get here so soon?'

'I padded the jolly old hoof most of the way.'

'No—I mean, what brought you here? I saw the girl write on the wall and came straight along, yet you are here as soon as I am.'

'A little bird whispered in my ear,' answered Bertie.

'You mean—the girl?'

'Oh, no. And the girl, my inquisitive partner, says she is a princess.'

'*The* princess?'

'Ah! There you have me. I'm no judge of princesses.'

The princess stepped into the conversation. She still carried her automatic. To Mario she said, 'Close the door and keep guard.' To the others she remarked, 'I am going to show you something. It may be what you are looking for. If it is, then all will be well. If you are spies, it will be a pity, because I shall have to shoot you. We take no risks.'

'No, by jingo, I can see that,' murmured Bertie.

The princess pushed aside an old wine press, disclosing a flight of steps leading downward. The pale yellow light of a candle came up the steps to meet the dim daylight in the kitchen. 'Descend,' she ordered. 'If you are recognised, all will be well. If not I shall be close behind you. Proceed.'

Algy went first. A dozen steps brought him to the bottom, into a bare, oblong cellar. There was only one piece of furniture, a wooden bedstead, on which a bed of dried herbs had been arranged. On it lay a man, a man whose emaciated face was half covered by a fortnight's stubble of beard. But the eyes that he turned on the visitors were clear. He was clad in an old boiler suit, but an R.A.F. uniform lay on the floor beside him.

Algy stopped. His heart appeared to seize up. 'Great heavens!' he breathed. 'Biggles!'

'Hello, boys,' answered Biggles. 'What are you staring at?'

'I—I hardly—knew you,' stammered Algy.

'Come right in, Bertie,' invited Biggles. 'Yes, I'm afraid I must look a bit of a mess, but I should have looked a lot worse by now had it not been for my nurse. Gentlemen, allow me to present to you Her Highness the Princess Marietta de Palma.'

The princess inclined her head and put away her pistol. 'So all is well,' she observed, speaking in English. 'Forgive me, but I had to be sure. There are more spies than scorpions in the country now.'

'How the deuce did you fellows find your way here?' demanded Biggles.

'When you didn't show up we twisted the story out of Raymond and he let us come down. We traced you by the writing on the wall,' explained Algy.

'Which means, I suppose, that Ginger is in the offing?'

'At the moment he's gone to a beastly place by the name of Peille,' put in Bertie.

'Why?' asked Biggles. Algy, too, looked surprised, for he knew nothing of Ginger's adventures.

'He went,' said Bertie, 'to get hold of Henri Ducoste, who is now a prisoner in the hospital at Peille.'

'Henri! A prisoner?—Peille—I don't understand! I assumed he got back to England?'

'He did. But he brought us over, and his engine let him down just after he had turned for home. He crashed between Peille and Baudon, and was taken to hospital pending removal to prison as a de Gaulleist*.'

'I didn't know anything about this,' Algy told Biggles helplessly.

'There are a lot of things you know nothing about, old boy,' continued Bertie. 'I'm a bit worried about Ginger. With one thing and another he may be in a mess. A bullet-hole in the leg has let a lot of the pink juice out of him.'

'Why didn't you go to Peille with him?' demanded Biggles.

'He said it would be better for me to come on here and try to make contact with Algy.'

'But how did you know I'd come here?' exclaimed Algy.

'Just a minute—just a minute,' broke in Biggles. 'We're all at sixes and sevens. Let's take things one at a time. I presume that you came over together and then got split up, so each doesn't know what the others have been doing?'

* Frenchman fighting under General de Gaulle against the Germans.

'That's about it,' agreed Bertie. 'But first of all, old boy, tell us about yourself. I hope you realise that until five minutes ago we didn't know whether you were alive or dead. Even Raymond didn't know, although in his heart he reckoned you were a gonner.'

Biggles smiled wanly. 'To tell the truth, I wasn't quite sure about it myself. The story won't take long. How much did Raymond tell you?'

Algy explained.

Biggles nodded. 'Well, as far as I can make out, what happened at Californie was this. I was making for the machine when a bullet hit me. Oh, yes, there was no fake about that. It knocked me for six. Actually the bullet hit a rib near the heart, glanced off and tore a hole in my side. The wound has healed up pretty well, but it kept me off my feet for a few days. The princess was already in the machine. When she saw me go down she jumped out again, with the result that the machine took off without either of us. Mind you, I didn't see this, because I was down for the count. Apparently there were a couple of Italians right on top of me. Her Highness, who carried a gun, shot them. There were some more on the way, so somehow or other she dragged me down to the sea, which was handy. The shock of the water brought me round, and for a little while I was able to take some slight interest in the proceedings. We lay there, the pair of us, with our noses just out of the water for about an hour, while the Italians searched high and low. When the excitement died away a bit we started making our way to Nice, half wading and half swimming. We managed to get to Jock's Bar, where I had already arranged for a blue message to be left—I'll explain about that later. It was my intention to write more, in case Raymond sent someone to look for us, but by that time I was all in. I'd lost rather more blood than the old system would stand.'

'I saw some of it,' murmured Algy.

'The princess got me inside,' resumed Biggles. 'She did a bit of first-aid work with some old bathing costumes, and then found herself with an unconscious man on her hands. Of course, she should have abandoned me and made for Spain—'

'I would not go over that again, my comrade,' broke in the princess. 'In my family we do not abandon our friends.'

Biggles smiled. 'That's the sort of girl she is,' he said softly, and then continued: 'Leaving me in Jock's Bar, she went back to Monaco, where she knew a chap who had once been in the Royal service. He ran a restaurant. As a matter of detail, I knew him myself—I'll explain how that came about presently.'

'That, I suppose, was Mario?' interposed Bertie. 'He put a knife into Zabani.'

'That was nothing to do with me,' asserted the princess. 'It was a crime of the Camorra. Zabani betrayed me. The Camorra had helped me to escape from Italy because it hates the Mussolini regime—and the Camorra never forgives or forgets.'

'Ginger got credit for killing Zabani, and it was in trying to get away that he was shot in the leg,' explained Bertie. 'But I'll tell you about that when my turn comes. Go ahead, chief.'

'Well, Mario turned up trumps,' resumed Biggles. 'As luck would have it, he happens to be in the local defence service as an ambulance driver. Having an empty garage, the ambulance is kept there. It was taking a chance, but he turned out and fetched me. I had no say in the matter, you understand, because all

166

this time I was unconscious. Mario and the princess fixed it between them. They brought me here. They daren't take me to the Chez Rossi in case someone spotted me being carried in—the place was fairly buzzing with police. Actually, Castillon was a good choice, because as the village has the reputation of being haunted, few people come near it. Mario knew of the place because once in a while he used to come over to gather the oranges and lemons that still grow in the gardens.'

'Yes, I know,' murmured Bertie dolefully. 'I hit the poor blighter in the eye with a lemon. I hope he won't hold it against me. Carry on, chief.'

'Well, that's really all there was to it. Princess Marietta stayed and nursed me while Mario kept us going with food. I recovered consciousness the day after they got me here, and I've been mending pretty fast ever since. We learned from Mario that someone was making inquiries, so I asked the princess to go down to Monaco again, to the Quai de Plaisance, and do a spot more writing on the wall, just in case Raymond had sent someone down to look for us. I gather that while she was writing she saw a bloke watching her, for which reason she left in such a hurry that she forgot the triangle.'

'I don't quite understand this,' put in Algy. 'Didn't you do any writing?'

'I'd better explain that,' answered Biggles. 'As it turned out, the blue pencil served its purpose, but at one time I was afraid it would do more harm than good. You see, most of the writing was done before the affair at Californie. When I arrived I went to the Villa Valdora, where I bumped into a man lurking in the bushes. That was Mario, who had somehow learned about the princess. We pretty soon saw eye to eye. He

167

told me that Zabani was a fascist, that the place was a trap, and that the princess had been taken to the police station at Monaco. Naturally, I couldn't let that stop me from trying to get her away, but my first thought, in case I failed, was to let Raymond's agents know, should they follow me, that the Villa Valdora was a place to avoid. I went to Mario's house to make my plans. I asked him to slip over to Nice and leave a message on the wall of Jock's Bar—which he did. While he was gone I wrote a message on the Pernod card in the restaurant, intending to go down to the Quai de Plaisance and leave a clue there. I wanted to put anyone who came—in case I failed—in touch with Mario, but I daren't say that in so many words. As it happened, I couldn't get to the Quai de Plaisance, and in point of fact nothing was written there until after the debacle of Californie. Later, when I woke up here in Castillon, I got the princess to slip down and write the message I had intended writing, to call attention to the Pernod card at Mario's. This morning, after I had learned definitely that someone had been making inquiries, I got her to go down again and write a new message, something more explicit. In the early messages I was only concerned with letting Raymond know that the Villa Valdora was a trap, and that Mario was a friend who could be relied on. Of course, I didn't know you'd be coming, but I thought Raymond might send someone. It wasn't easy, with the police fairly on the hop, to write messages in such a way that they would look pointless to anyone but the people for whom they were intended.'

'It was the word Mayday that set me thinking,' asserted Bertie.

'I used the word deliberately to show that there was

a hook-up with aviation,' rejoined Biggles. 'Mario is a good lad, but if anything he tends to be over suspicious. He was concerned only with the princess, and he was all against taking chances. As far as he was concerned, everyone was a spy. All the same, I must say you weren't long picking up the trail. Frankly, I hadn't much hope of getting away from here by air, so we were making other plans, using Mario's ambulance— but never mind about that for the moment. What about you?'

Algy told his story first, describing his visit to Jock's Bar. 'Someone must have found the bloodstained rags, and told the police to put them on the scent,' he declared. 'Gordino was there, waiting for someone to turn up, and he nearly got me.' He then narrated the story of his journey to Monaco, how he had seen the girl in blue on the Quai de Plaisance, and how he had made his way to Castillon. He concluded by informing Biggles of the stirring events in North Africa which had resulted in the enemy occupation of the whole of France. The Italians, he asserted, were as thick as ants along the Riviera.

'Not Italians, please,' corrected the princess. 'You mean the dupes of Mussolini—that rat of the Romagnna.'

'That's the way it is,' said Biggles sadly. 'The princess hates Mussolini even more than we do. And she's not the only one to detest that puffed-up gangster. But what happened to you, Bertie?'

Bertie told his story and followed it up by telling Ginger's, up to the point where they had parted in the house of Madame Ducoste at Monaco.

Biggles heard him out in silence. 'We must get in touch with Ginger and Henri right away,' he decided.

'This attempted rescue sounds a formidable business to me. When we've done that we'll see about getting home.'

'What I'm anxious to know is, how are you feeling?' asked Algy.

The princess answered. 'He gets well quickly because of the good constitution, but he is not strong yet.'

'I'm getting stronger every day,' declared Biggles. 'I got up for a couple of hours yesterday, and I've been walking up and down this cellar most of the morning. All I really need is a bath and a shave. The bath will have to wait, but Mario has promised to bring me a razor.'

'Are you kidding about feeling all right?' asked Algy suspiciously.

'No, I'm all right now, as long as I don't put any great strain on my side, which might open up the wound. The princess is a great nurse—and she can cook.'

'By Jove! Really?' murmured Bertie.

'What was this plan for getting away, the one you spoke about just now?' inquired Algy.

'Briefly, it was this,' answered Biggles. 'We thought we'd have a shot at getting to the Spanish frontier. The idea was, Mario would bring the ambulance along here. He would drive it, wearing his uniform. The princess would get herself up as a nurse, and I, as the patient—an Italian officer wounded in the Western Desert. We couldn't hope to get all the way to Spain in the ambulance, because of the petrol shortage, but we thought we might at least get clear of the Riviera, which is the real danger zone.'

Algy shook his head. 'That might have been all right last week, but I don't think it would work now; the

Riviera is stiff with Italian troops, and the Nazis have taken over farther along the coast—Toulon and Marseilles. You would be stopped, and without papers what story could you tell? What reason could Mario give for being so far from Monaco?'

Biggles was silent for a little while. 'Yes, I'm afraid this invasion has altered things,' he agreed. 'Still, it's worth bearing in mind that Mario can get transport if it comes to the pinch. But it's no use talking about that until we've got hold of Ginger and Henri. I'm worried about them. I'm afraid I can't do much about it myself. Neither can the princess, and Mario will have to look after the food department. What time is it?'

Mario, from the cellar steps, answered, 'It is seven o'clock, *signor*, and a fine night.'

'I didn't know he spoke English,' said Algy in surprise.

'He was in London for a while—had a little restaurant in Soho,' explained Biggles.

'Well, what are we going to do?' inquired Bertie. 'Shall we—that is, me and Algy—toddle along to Peille, to see what is happening there?'

'What was your final arrangement with Ginger?'

'He said he'd get hold of Henri and make for here.'

'H'm. That makes it hard to know what to do for the best. He may already be on his way here. If you go, whichever way you take, you may miss him. At all costs we must try to keep together.'

'It is possible, *signor*, to getta from here to Peille by the ancient mule tracks,' alleged Mario. 'All the old villages are so joined up.'

'You know the path?

'Ah, no. I notta go that way.'

'Then you couldn't be sure of finding the path in the dark?'

'No, *signor*. In daylight, perhaps.'

Biggles thought for a moment. 'I don't see that we can do anything until morning,' he decided. 'If we start blundering about in the dark we may do more harm than good. We'll wait and give Ginger a chance to get here, in case he's on the way. If he isn't here by dawn, then someone will have to take the mountain path to Peille, while another watches the Sospel road to see if he comes that way. After all, we're not tied to time. You fellows must be tired after all your running about. I suggest you make yourselves comfortable—or as comfortable as you can—until morning. Then we'll make a definite plan. Mario has brought plenty of food, so we shan't starve.'

'And is Mario to stay here also?' asked the princess.

'Yes. I think he'd better wait in case we need him,' answered Biggles. 'For the moment he had better remain on guard, in case anyone comes snooping round—not that I think it's likely.'

And so it was arranged.

Chapter 15
Conference at Castillon

Just as dawn was breaking Mario came into the wine cellar where Biggles, Algy and Bertie were sleeping, and having apologized for awakening them, announced that someone, he knew not who, was approaching from the south-west. This, he asserted, was beyond dispute, because on three occasions he had distinctly heard a stone rattle, and each time the sound was nearer. The intervals between the sounds had been long, from which it might be inferred that the approach was slow. He had come to warn them to be ready for action, and to ask for instructions.

Biggles turned to Algy and Bertie. 'You'd better take care of this,' he ordered. 'Don't show yourselves. Try an ambush. Probably the best plan would be to take cover in a house on the line of approach, so that before you move you can see who you have to deal with. Speaking personally, if it is the police, I am not going to be taken prisoner—I'd sooner fight it out here than face a firing squad. Have you got guns?'

'We have,' answered Algy grimly. 'Come on, Bertie.'

Under the guidance of Mario they made their way to the outskirts of the village and entered an empty house, a window of which commanded a view over the direction from which danger threatened. Dawn was now advancing with a rush, the rising sun turning the surrounding peaks to gold, and drowning the morning star in a sea of turquoise, pink and mauve.

For a few minutes nothing could be seen, and then, from a fold in the ground, appeared a brown object, which presently resolved itself into the head of a donkey, walking very slowly. As the animal came into full view two figures could be seen, one, in pale blue overalls, slumped on its back, the other leaning wearily against it.

'Good heavens!' muttered Algy. 'It's Ginger. By thunder! He's got Henri.'

'Yes, by jingo, you're right—absolutely right,' said Bertie in a startled voice.

With one accord they dashed to the door and raced towards the little party as fast as the state of the ground would permit.

Ginger heard them, and looked up to see them coming. He waved a greeting. 'Hello chaps, glad to see you,' he said, smiling. 'Look after Henri—he's in a bad way.'

'You look all in, yourself,' observed Algy, giving him an arm.

'I'm all right—just tired,' murmured Ginger. 'Henri is hurt, though.' Suddenly noticing Mario advancing he groped for his gun. 'Strewth, what's that fellow doing here?'

'He's all right—he's one of us,' answered Algy.

'But that's the bloke who knifed Zabani.'

'So what? Zabani only got what was coming to him. Believe it or not, Mario is on our side.'

Ginger shook his head. 'I'll take your word for it. After the last twenty-four hours I'll believe anything.'

Algy spoke to Mario. 'Run back and let them know it's Ginger and Henri arrived,' he ordered, and then devoted his attention to getting the casualties into the village.

174

Ginger was able to walk, but Henri was too far gone. He was conscious, but only just. Even the donkey seemed exhausted.

'We've had a longish hike,' explained Ginger. 'These rocks are the very deuce. They've worn the soles clean off my feet.' He said nothing about his wounded leg.

'Never mind, old boy,' put in Bertie. 'We've got a tonic waiting for you—yes, by jingo, not half.'

'What is it?'

'Biggles.'

Ginger stopped, his eyes saucering. 'What? You mean that?'

'Absolutely.'

'Then he's okay after all.'

'He looks as though he could do with a top overhaul, otherwise he's all right,' asserted Algy. 'The princess is here, too.'

'Well, knock me down with a blanket! That's the tops!' cried Ginger delightedly, quickening his pace.

'Wait till you see the princess—she's a wizard.'

'I'm not interested in princesses,' declared Ginger casually.

'She saved Biggles.'

'He saved her first, so what about it?' inquired Ginger. 'There's only one girl I want to see. . . .'

'Oh, good lor! Haven't you forgotten her yet?' lamented Bertie.

Ginger glared. 'What do you mean—forgotten her?' he demanded harshly.

'What *is* this?' interposed Algy.

'Henri's sister, Jeanette, has shot poor old Ginger to bits,' explained Bertie sadly.

Ginger tapped Bertie on the chest with an irate, and very dirty, finger. 'Listen, my noble comrade. . . .'

Algy stopped the argument. He could see trouble brewing. 'All right, no more talking,' he broke in tersely. 'Wait till we get inside.'

This did not take long. Mario took Lucille to a stable, promising to feed and water her. Ginger walked and Henri was carried, into the cellar.

Biggles was up, and smiling. He greeted Ginger warmly, but was too concerned about Henri to go into immediate explanations. He asked the princess to examine the sick man, which she did with semi-professional ability, removing the bandages from his head to look at the wound. When she had finished, and had rebandaged Henri's head, she took Biggles on one side.

'He is bad,' she said. 'The wound is clean, and seems to be healing, but it will take time. Also, he suffers from shock. This journey has made great demands on his strength. Only his will kept him going for so long. What he needs is rest, and, of course, most of all, a doctor.'

'A doctor!' cried Biggles in dismay. 'There's no hope of that here—unless we hand him back to the police, and that, in the long run, would do him more harm than good. We shall have to do what we can for him here—at any rate, until we see how he shapes. With one thing and another we're a pretty groggy lot. How about you, Ginger?'

'Oh, I'm all right,' replied Ginger lightly. 'That hike across the mountains, coming on top of everything else, sort of emptied my reserve tanks, but they're filling up again now. You don't look as smart yourself as I have seen you look.'

'I'm on my feet, at all events,' answered Biggles, smiling. 'Let me introduce you to the Princess Marietta de Palma.'

176

The princess gave Ginger her hand, with a smile. 'Your commandant has often spoken of you during the long while we have been here. I am happy to meet his friends. Forgive me, now, I must get back to my patient.'

While the princess was making Henri as comfortable as possible on the bed recently vacated by Biggles, Ginger told his story. 'We were doing fine till we were nearly here, then poor old Henri began to fold up,' he concluded. 'All I need is a rest, but I'm afraid Henri needs more than that. He pretended he was all right, and I didn't realize how sick he was until he collapsed. That mule track was no macadam highway.'

Mario appeared. 'I makka da soup, and da *spaghetti alla Napoletana*,' he announced.

The princess got up from the bedside. 'With food and rest he will improve, but he really should have a doctor. I will help Mario with the soup.' She went up the steps to the kitchen.

'This is some princess,' remarked Ginger as she disappeared. 'She can nurse, and apparently she can cook.'

'Princess Marietta is the real thing,' declared Biggles. 'She's been wonderful.'

'Here, I say, this is getting a bit thick,' muttered Bertie, polishing his eyeglass furiously. 'First Jeanette, now a bally princess. I don't hold with all these women in the party.'

'There are only two, so far,' returned Biggles blandly.

Bertie shook his head sadly. 'Women and planes don't mix. I once had a pal, a jolly good pilot, too, who walked straight into a spinning airscrew. He was looking at a gal who had just stepped on the tarmac.

That's the sort of thing that happens—if you see what I mean?'

'Oh, go and play yourself a tune,' murmured Ginger.

'What would be more to the point,' suggested Biggles, 'let's get together and talk things over. But I'll tell you this,' he added. 'Since meeting Princess Marietta my opinion of princesses has touched a new altitude record.'

'Suppose we cut out this romancing and get down to brass tacks?' broke in Algy. 'We've got to get Henri a doctor, and we shan't get one here. We've also to get ourselves home, and that—forgive me if I appear pessimistic—doesn't look easy. Start thinking, somebody, and think fast.'

'Here's Mario—let's have some breakfast first,' proposed Biggles, as Mario and the princess appeared with dishes, plates and cups.

'This war gets curiouser and curiouser—if you get my meaning?' remarked Bertie. 'A couple of days ago Mario tried to bump me into a gorge; now he's feeding me with soup. I'm all for getting back into the air where I can see where I'm going.'

'What about Biggles being saved by an enemy princess?' queried Ginger. 'That takes a bit of swallowing.'

'That's where you're wrong,' disputed Biggles. 'Princess Marietta isn't an enemy. She isn't even Italian. She's a Sicilian—so is Mario. Apparently there is a difference. Anyway, you wouldn't expect a princess to take orders from a puffed-up scallywag of the Romagna—that's what the princess calls Mussolini—who murdered her father. But shut up—here she is.'

Breakfast over, the dishes were collected by Mario, who disappeared with them up the stairs. A moment later, as the others were about to settle down to talk, he reappeared, beckoning excitedly.

'Come,' he said. 'Many aeroplanes.'

They all hastened up the steps and followed the waiter into the open. It was now broad day. But Ginger was not concerned with that. His nerves thrilled as he heard the familiar drone of aircraft.

'There they are, coming up from Italy—' said Biggles, pointing to the south east. 'One, two, three . . . twelve of them. Savoia flying-boats. Must be a squadron on the move. Wonder where they're bound for?'

'Part of the new occupation outfit, I reckon,' suggested Ginger.

'They're losing height,' observed Biggles. 'They're already over Mentone so they're not going there. I should say it's Monaco, Nice, or possibly Cannes— there's a harbour at each place.'

For a few minutes they watched in silence, watched while the drone of the engines died away and the gliding angle of the aircraft steepened.

'Monaco,' said Biggles. 'Now if only we could get hold of one of those babies. . . .'

'Why not?' murmured Ginger.

'Upon my life, the boy's getting positively reckless,' asserted Bertie.

'If we don't fly it means we've either got to walk or swim, and it's a long trip, either way,' declared Ginger. 'Apart from which, we're getting such a big party that we could hardly hope to stroll away without being noticed.'

'Flying would suit me nicely,' interposed Algy. 'You grab one of those machines and you can reckon on me as a passenger.'

'That's enough fooling,' put in Biggles quietly.

'Ginger was right when he said we are a long way from the nearest friendly frontier. We can't sit here indefinitely; on the other hand, none of us is really in a fit state to tackle a six or seven hundred mile jaunt. Henri's condition rules that out, anyway. We've got to get transport of some sort. Admittedly, Mario has an ambulance, and it might get us a little way, but as soon as we ran out of petrol, which is almost impossible to get here, we should be cheesed. An aircraft would suit us admirably, but experience has shown that it isn't as easy to snatch a machine in enemy country as some people seem to think. All the same, the possibilities are worth exploring.'

'I should have thought,' resumed Ginger, 'that the risks of trying to get a plane were no greater than trying to get across the frontier into Spain or Switzerland, the only neutral countries within reach without crossing water. Suppose I go down to Monaco to find out just what the chances of pinching a plane look like?'

'Wait a minute, that's my pigeon,' protested Bertie.

'Why yours?'

'Because I've got a useful pal on the spot—my old boatman, François Budette.'

'All right, let's both go,' agreed Ginger. 'I want to go to Monaco, anyway.'

Bertie groaned. 'It's that girl again.'

'Not at all,' argued Ginger. 'As far as Henri's mother is concerned, Henri is in jail at Nice, waiting to be shot. She helped me in the preparations for the rescue, so the least we can do is let her know that Henri is safe, so far. Of course, if I saw Jeanette at the same time I should speak to her—out of common politeness.'

'Why this sudden passion for good behaviour?' sneered Algy.

'I think Ginger's right about *madame*,' put in Biggles.
'We must let her know about Henri. But are you in a
fit state, Ginger, to walk to Monaco? Don't forget the
police are waiting for you.'

'I never felt better in my life,' declared Ginger. 'And
as far as the police are concerned—well, that goes for
all of us. I've got Lucille to ride on, don't forget.'

'Like you, she needs a rest,' Biggles pointed out.

'To save much trouble, suppose Mario went and
fetched his ambulance?' suggested the princess. 'Then
you could both ride down. And if you went inside you
would be out of sight.'

'That sounds better,' assented Biggles. 'If there's
going to be transport I'll go down and have a look at
things myself. How does Mario feel about it?'

The princess consulted Mario in rippling Italian.

'He says he thinks it might be done,' she informed
the others. 'He's willing to try. But unless he is able to
get a lift into Monaco it will be late in the afternoon
before he can get back.'

'Now we're getting somewhere,' breathed Ginger
enthusiastically.

'Actually, I should be the one to go with Biggles and
Bertie,' said Algy.

'Not on your life,' denied Ginger. 'You don't even
know where Madamé Ducoste lives—I do.'

'Okay, Romeo,' submitted Algy, grinning.

'I think it's a deplorable thing that a fellow can't
have a platonic friendship without these lousy insin-
uations,' snorted Ginger bitterly.

'All right, laddie, put your hackles down,' consoled
Biggles. 'Mario had better get off right away. When he
comes back he will have to stop at the nearest point
on the Sospel road. We'll be on the watch for him.'

Mario went off, and the others settled down to discuss their adventures in more detail. Princess Marietta sat by Henri's bed and gave him water from time to time. It was obvious that his head wound was troubling him.

At noon they started to look out for Mario, not that they expected him back so soon, but Biggles was leaving nothing to chance; and as it transpired he was right, for a few minutes after Algy—who had volunteered for the first watch—had taken up his position, he saw a covered vehicle, bearing the red and white colours of the Principality of Monaco, coming up the slope. He hurried back to the cellar and informed the others of its arrival.

Biggles, dressed only in his boiler suit, at once prepared to depart. With Bertie and Ginger he went down to the car, which had already been turned, to find Mario at the wheel looking very smart in his uniform. At his suggestion they lay inside on the stretchers. As he closed the door he explained that his quick return was due to his having got a lift on a military lorry from Mentone to Monaco. The flying-boats, he stated, were in the harbour.

The journey to Monaco was made without incident beyond occasional hold-ups due to the congested state of the road. It may have been as a result of the heavy traffic, which kept the police busy, that the ambulance was allowed to pass without question. Mario stopped at the end of the Boulevard des Moulins rather than risk running down the hill to the Condamine where he could be seen by the palace guards, who might ask him why he had brought the ambulance out.

'Now I put da ambulance in my garage,' said Mario.

'I pick you up here to take you back—in one hour, yes?'

'That should be ample time for what we want to do,' agreed Biggles, and Mario drove on.

They were proceeding on their way to the harbour when their attention was attracted by a little group of people standing in front of the official notice board at the bottom of the casino gardens.

'Let's see what it's all about,' suggested Ginger.

'Probably the names of the winners in the latest lottery,' predicted Bertie.

'We'll just have a glance in case it affects us,' decided Biggles, glancing round. There were one or two police about, but they were swamped in the tide of Italian troops. Convoys had parked beside the road and soldiers were everywhere, talking and smoking.

They all walked over to read the notice, which they found had been printed in both French and Italian, under the Italian flag.

As Ginger read it his body seemed to go cold, and his nerves to contract. For the notice concerned them very closely. In the first paragraph it promised a reward of ten thousand francs to anyone submitting information which would lead to the arrest of Henri Ducoste, described as a rebel and a de Gaulleist. But it was not that which shook Ginger, and gave him a sinking feeling in the pit of his stomach. It was the last paragraph. This asserted that if the reward was not claimed, and if Henri had not delivered himself up within twenty-four hours, his mother and sister, Madame and Mademoiselle Ducoste, of Monaco, would be arrested as hostages, and summarily shot. The signature at the bottom was Signor Gregori Gordino, prefect of the special police.

Biggles nudged Ginger's arm. 'Don't speak a word,' he cautioned. 'Let's get out of the crowd.'

Chapter 16
Biggles Takes Over

Ginger walked on down the hill behind Biggles. His face was white with passion.

'The swine,' he muttered incoherently. 'The unutterable swine. Can you beat that? They'd shoot two women because. . . .'

'Take it easy, or you'll have people looking at you,' warned Biggles. 'Let's stop here for a moment and calm down.' He halted by the sea wall which, from a hundred feet above, looked down on the little harbour.

Bertie joined them. He, too, was pale and his eyes glittered frostily. 'That's a bit steep,' he muttered. 'Absolutely vertical, in fact.'

Ginger nearly choked. 'Oh for a Lancaster,' he grated. 'I'd fan this place flat.'

'And kill a lot of perfectly innocent people,' said Biggles bitingly. 'You're out of control, get back on your course.'

'If Henri hears about this he'll give himself up,' averred Bertie.

'Let us hope that he doesn't hear about it.'

'In which case,' rejoined Ginger harshly, 'Jeanette and her mother will be shot by this viper Gordino.'

'Oh, stop bleating,' snapped Biggles. 'They aren't shot yet, and we've ample time to do something.'

'Do what? What can we do? Now that notice has been posted, the Rue Marinière will be watched by the

185

police to make sure that Jeanette and her mother don't try to get away.'

Biggles lit a cigarette and flicked the match over the balustrade. 'You're working yourself into a sweat and the mascara is running out of your hair down your face,' he observed. 'Wipe it off—unless you're trying to camouflage yourself as a zebra.'

'Okay—okay. But what are we going to do?' implored Ginger.

Biggles jerked his thumb towards the old village of Monaco, on the far side of the harbour. 'You see that rock over there?'

'Yes.'

'You see the castle on it?'

'Of course.'

Biggles turned and pointed to the east, where, at no great distance, the coast of Italy jutted out into the sea. 'There's a town there called Ventimiglia,' he said casually. 'About seven hundred years ago a lad named Francis Grimaldi lived there. One day he woke up feeling very much as you do now. You see, the bloke who lived at the castle here at Monaco, a skunk named Spinola, had pinched his girl and locked her in the tower. Grimaldi didn't stand and swear—or if he did there's no record of it. As soon as it was dark he put his knife in his belt, coiled a rope round his waist, and rowing up to the rock, he scaled the cliff. Slitting the throats of people who were foolish enough to ask him where he was going, he went along to the castle, where, in the main hall, Spinola was guzzling wine with a party of pals. Grimaldi locked the door and set the place on fire. With his rope he rescued his girl, lowered her into the boat and returned home. So they lived happily ever after. You may have noticed that the street through the Condamine is named Rue Grimaldi. Now, the point of my story is this. If Grimaldi could do a show like that and get away with it, in comparison our job of fetching Mrs and Miss Ducoste from the Rue Marinière looks easy—don't you agree?'

Ginger grinned sheepishly. 'Sorry. Go ahead.'

'Of course, we can't just drop what we came here to do, so we shall have to try to do both,' resumed Biggles. 'Let's get organized. It means breaking up the party. Bertie, I shall have to ask you to get all the gen about the aircraft. Go and see François and find out what he knows. I shall want you to tell me how long the machines are here for, how they are moored, if they are guarded, and so on. You've got an hour to do it in. In one hour from now be at the corner of the Bou des Moulins, where Mario dropped us just now. We'll pick you up there. If we're delayed, wait. Got that?'

Bertie nodded. 'Absolutely.'

'Fine. Get cracking.'

Bertie turned away. 'See you later.'

'And now what do we do?' asked Ginger anxiously.

'For a start, instead of looking like a couple of tramps, we've got to get ourselves up to look like important people—Italian officers, for instance. Yes—that should be easy. I can see quite a lot of troops bathing in the harbour, and more are going down. Let's join them.'

Ginger stared. 'Are you crazy?'

'Possibly, but I hope not,' answered Biggles. 'We're not actually going to bathe, of course; pleasant though it would be, we've hardly time for that. But the idea gives us a perfectly good reason for taking off our clothes. See those two officers going down with towels? They're just about our weight. They'll probably be in the water for half an hour. When they dive in the drink, we'll dive into their uniforms.'

'And then?'

'We'll go up to the Chez Rossi, get Mario to turn out his blood-wagon, proceed to the Rue Marinière, and arrest Madame and Mademoiselle Ducoste. We shall then return to Castillon, taking the ladies with us, collecting Bertie on the way. Of course, it may not work out quite as smoothly as that, but that's the general idea.'

'Okay, let's get going.'

As they walked down the hill Ginger asked, 'If we can get these uniforms, what happens if anyone speaks to us in Italian?'

'We just act as if we didn't hear 'em,' answered Biggles calmly.

The first part of the programme worked out so easily that Ginger found it hard not to smile. The two Italian officers joined the crowd of bathers on the quay and started to undress. Biggles and Ginger, taking up a position near them, followed suit. The Italians dived into the sea. Biggles and Ginger walked forward and dressed in their clothes. There were not fewer than a hundred Italians dressing and undressing at the time, and in such a crowd it was a simple matter to effect the change without comment. It was all done in less than five minutes. Without undue haste they turned away and walked up the hill.

'Whatever happens, it should take those fellows quite a while to work out that their togs have really been pinched,' remarked Biggles. 'It will probably be the last thing they think of. They'll suppose their kit has got mixed up with other people's.' Biggles returned the salute of two more Italian soldiers going down to bathe.

Nobody spoke to them. Nobody appeared to take the slightest notice of them, which, as Biggles pointed out, since nobody knew them was a reasonable expectation. It would be sheer bad luck if they were accosted by an officer senior to themselves, although they were only lieutenants. They reached the Chez Rossi without trouble, and found Mario in the kitchen, washing dishes. He nearly dropped one when Biggles and Ginger walked in through the side door.

'It's all right, Mario, don't get excited,' said Biggles quietly. 'Madame Ducoste and her daughter are to be arrested as hostages if Henri doesn't give himself up. We've got to get them away before that can happen. The only place we can take them is Castillon, and the only way we can get them there is in your ambulance. Get it out. Then all you have to do is drive us straight to the Rue Marinière—that is, if you want to get your princess out of the country.'

'*Si—si, signor*.' Mario nearly fell over himself in his haste to get into his uniform tunic, which he had only just taken off. It was hanging behind the door. From time to time he muttered and shrugged his shoulders as though he found it hard to keep pace with events.

Biggles and Ginger went with him to the garage and sat with him on the front seat. Without speaking, but with a slightly dazed expression on his face, he drove to the Rue Marinière. Two soldiers were standing at the end of the street, smoking. They straightened themselves and saluted the officers as the ambulance went past without stopping. A Monégasque policeman was sitting in a chair at the door of number six. He stood up.

'Tell him,' said Biggles to Mario, 'that we have orders to arrest the occupants of this house.'

189

The *gendarme* did not question this. Possibly he expected it. After all, the Italians had taken charge of the principality. In fact, he looked relieved that responsibility was being taken off his shoulders.

Ginger knocked at the door. It was opened by Madame Ducoste. Ginger went in, followed by Biggles. As soon as they were inside he closed the door. Madame Ducoste clutched at her throat and uttered a little cry when, looking at Ginger's face, she suddenly recognized him.

'Where is Jeanette?' asked Ginger tersely.

'She is upstairs.'

'Fetch her, please. Time is short.'

Madame ran up the stairs and returned with Jeanette, looking not a little startled. Her eyes were red as though with weeping.

'Now listen carefully, *madame*,' went on Ginger. 'All is well. Don't be alarmed.'

'But we are in great trouble, *monsieur*,' broke in *madame*.

'Yes, we know all about it—that's why we are here. Henri is safe. We have him with us in the mountains.'

'Thank God.'

'He is hurt, but not seriously. If he gives himself up he will be shot. If he does not give himself up, you will be shot. There is only one way of escape. Come with us and we will take you to him. Afterwards we shall all go to England. But this you must understand. If you decide to come with us you must be prepared to abandon everything. We have no time for baggage. Now, *madame*, the choice is yours. Shall Henri give himself up? Will you submit to arrest, or will you throw in your lot with us—and Henri?'

190

Jeanette's eyes were on her mother's face. 'Let us go,' she breathed. 'It is the only way.'

'We will go with you, *monsieur*,' decided *madame*. 'I must be with my boy. If we are to die, then we will die together.'

'Bravely spoken, *madame*,' put in Biggles. 'That is what we hoped you would say. Are you ready?'

'We are in your hands, under God, *monsieur*.'

Ginger opened the door. To his alarm a little crowd had collected, but its sympathy, as was to be expected, was with the two women—their own folk.

'Say nothing, *madame*. Look as though you are resigned to being arrested,' said Biggles quietly as he opened the rear of the ambulance and helped them in.

There was some hissing and hooting. A stone was thrown.

Ginger got in with the two prisoners. Biggles slammed the door and went round to the front, to Mario, who sat like a graven image on his seat.

'Drive on, Mario,' ordered Biggles as he got in.

To a chorus of shouts and curses the car went down the narrow street with Mario sounding his horn to clear a path through the swiftly growing crowd before the anger of which the two Italian soldiers were beating a hasty retreat. For a moment or two it looked as though there was going to be a riot, which was something Biggles had not foreseen, and which was the last thing he wanted. However, the car got clear of the street and Mario sped on down the long ramp that leads to the Condamine. Straight through the Boulevard Albert behind the harbour he drove, and up the incline to Monte Carlo.

'Stop at the place where you dropped us this morning,' ordered Biggles. 'We have someone to pick up.'

191

A few seconds later the corner came into sight. Bertie was waiting, making music to an admiring gathering of urchins.

'Get in the back,' called Biggles.

Without a word Bertie got in. The door slammed. The car went on.

After that, on the whole, progress was good, although there was one nasty moment in a traffic hold-up, when Biggles saw a Monégasque *gendarme* regarding the vehicle curiously. Mario noticed it, too. Instead of waiting, he turned out of the queue and took a turning to the right, to the lower road, at the end of which a left turn brought him back to the main thoroughfare. There was still a certain amount of traffic coming from Italy, but it had thinned out considerably and Mario was able to maintain a good speed.

On reaching Mentone there was another hold-up at the Sospel turning. The road, a sentry insisted, was closed. This came as no surprise. But as there was no other road within miles of Castillon, Mario had to take a chance. He did it well.

'Fool!' he shouted. 'Can't you see that this is an ambulance? There has been trouble. We have orders to fetch a wounded man.'

The sentry apologized and waved them on.

On the long pull up the mountain road Biggles had a serious talk with Mario. He realized that the restaurant owner's only real interest in the affair was his attachment to the princess and his secret society. He probably hated fascism, anyway, on the principle that most Sicilians hate any form of government which must inevitably exercise restraint—as against complete freedom of action. Hence the numerous secret societies which exist on the island.

Biggles apologized for having got Mario involved in his affairs, pointing out frankly that he feared this latest escapade would make it difficult for him to return to Monaco.

Mario stated with equal frankness that he was quite sure of it. It would be known that his ambulance had been used for the rescue. The police in Monaco, to say nothing of half the people, had seen him. He had also been observed by the *gendarme* at the traffic hold-up.

'If you go back to Monaco you will be arrested,' predicted Biggles.

Mario answered—somewhat surprisingly, Biggles thought—that he had no intention of going back to Monaco. It was not outside the bounds of possibility that the secret police would discover that he had killed Zabani. He had always been suspected of being a Camorrista, and the paper on the dagger would tell them that the crime was an act of vengeance by the Camorra. In any case, he said, the little business he had spent years working up had been ruined by the war. 'How,' he asked plaintively, taking his hands off the wheel to lend expression to his words, 'How can a man run a restaurant when there is nothing to cook?'

Biggles admitted that as a problem the question did present difficulties.

'What does it matter?' rejoined Mario, with true Latin philosophy. 'I would rather serve the princess. If she will have me, I will stay with her and go where she goes. It may be that there will be some more traitors to kill,' he added hopefully.

This decision simplified Biggles' immediate problem. 'We hope the princess will go to England with us,' he announced. 'Would you follow her there?'

Mario drew a deep breath. 'Yes, I would follow her

even to England. For her I will suffer the rain and the fog,' he announced in a tone of voice which left Biggles in no doubt as to his opinion of the English climate.

'To-night we shall try to escape in an aeroplane,' continued Biggles. 'I have a plan. If we decide on it, will you drive the party down to the sea?'

'Why should I mind? There is enough petrol. There is even a spare can, not yet opened. I am told that if I open it I shall be sent to prison; but as I shall be shot now if they catch me, how can they send me to prison for opening the petrol?'

'How, indeed?' murmured Biggles. 'It was clever of you to think of that.'

'Thank you, *signor*,' answered Mario simply.

'The question is, what shall we do with the ambulance when we get to Castillon?'

'What shall we do with it?'

'That's what I'm asking you. We can't leave it standing on the road. Could we get up the track to the village?'

'Who knows?'

'I thought perhaps you might,' replied Biggles softly. There were times when he found Mario's Latin habit of answering a question with a question rather trying. 'Well, see what you can do about it. We've got to get it off the road,' he concluded.

Arriving at the end nearest to Castillon, Mario got the vehicle off the road by the simple expedient of charging the hillside, with a fine disregard for tyres, springs and passengers. 'The ambulance doesn't belong to me,' he explained in reply to a questioning look from Biggles. With the engine racing in bottom gear the car crashed and banged its way over the rocks, and finally bounced into the village street.

'No one will see it here unless a person comes to the village,' announced Mario carelessly. 'If a person comes –*tch*,' he touched his stiletto.

Biggles dismounted, and going to the rear of the vehicle, found Bertie and Ginger, with their charges, getting out.

'For the moment you are safe, *madame*,' he said with a smile of confidence. 'Come with me and I will take you to Henri.'

The others followed.

Chapter 17
Plan For Escape

The reunion of Henri and his family, whom he had not seen for three years, gave Ginger an idea of the mental anguish hundreds of thousands of people, parted by the war and unable to get in touch with each other, were suffering. It made any risks they had taken more than worth while. After watching them for a minute, Biggles beckoned to the others to follow him up to the kitchen, where, without preamble, he asked Bertie to report the result of his reconnaissance at the harbour.

'First I had a talk with François,' began Bertie. 'From the window of his house I could see everything that was going on, so the whole show was really a slice of pie. François, by the way, is all against these beastly fascists who have made a mucker of jolly old Monaco. He'll do anything to annoy them, and as he has the boat he may be useful. It's my old racer, you know. I've told him he can have it—it'll be out of date for racing by the time the war is over.'

'Does the engine still function?' put in Biggles.

'Well, old boy, it would if it had any petrol. François is a first-class mechanic, which is why I employed him in the old days, and as he couldn't bear to see the engine go to bits he has kept it on the top line—if you see what I mean? Not being able to use the motor, he's rigged up a sail for waffling up and down the coast looking after his lobster pots, which is about as much fishing as he does. By the way, he has a licence from the authorities to go fishing, so everyone is accustomed to see him pottering in and out of the harbour. We talked over the possibility of sailing to Spain, but we decided it was too far—eight hundred miles or thereabouts. *Bluebird* is purely a racer, with no keel and a very shallow draft; without power she couldn't live five minutes in a heavy sea. The Gulf of Lyons can be the very devil in a westerly gale, should we be caught out. Moreover, she was designed as a two-seater, but François has taken off most of the faring, so she would carry eight or nine people for a short distance in a calm sea.'

'That's useful to know,' murmured Biggles. 'What about the aircraft?'

'There are twelve Savoias in the harbour, moored to buoys in three lines of four—as you probably saw for yourself?' continued Bertie. 'The leading machine of the outside line carries a pennant, so presumably it's the C.O.'s* kite. The officers are living in the Bristol hotel, just opposite, and the crews are parked in the Beau Rivage, at the bottom of the hill. As far as I could make out there are no sentries except a headquarter guard in the custom-house; but if I know anything about the Ities they probably spend most of their time playing cards. I don't suppose it would occur to them that someone might borrow one of the machines. There are a fair number of troops round the harbour, bathing and what not. I gather from François that it goes on half the night. I've saved the most important spot of news still last. I didn't hear this myself, but an Italian told François that the squadron leaves to-morrow for a secret destination, which I wasn't able to discover.'

* Commanding Officer

197

'It doesn't matter two hoots where they're going,' observed Biggles thoughtfully. 'But if they're pushing off to-morrow it means that as far as we're concerned to-night's the night. What time are they going?'

'I couldn't find out. There seems to be some doubt about it.'

'No matter. They'll hardly be likely to move before daylight, and by that time our show will be over, one way or the other. Did you hear of any particular reason why they stopped here?'

'François thinks it was something to do with fuel—at least he heard them talking about oil and petrol.'

'Thanks, Bertie. You've done a good job. Now let us see how the show lines up. We've got quite a large party. Mario has decided to come with us, so that will make nine all told. As far as the aircraft is concerned, that's all right; a dozen people could pack into one of those Savoias. Our big difficulty will be Henri. He'll have to be carried. All the same, with reasonable luck I think we ought to be able to pull this off. The Italians are an easy-going lot—thank goodness.'

Biggles thought for a little while, gazing at the floor. Then he looked up. 'All right,' he resumed. 'Listen carefully, everybody. This is my scheme, and success, as usual, will depend on perfect timing. The moon is due to show just before three, so our best time for action will be a trifle before that. What I mean is, we should have darkness when we want it, and afterwards, when a spot of light would be useful, we shall have the moon.'

'We're still wearing Italian uniforms, don't forget,' interposed Ginger. 'How does that work in?'

'So much the better for the scheme I have in mind. Our two most useful assets are Mario's ambulance and

François' boat. I'm adapting the show to use them both. Mario tells me he is all right for petrol. This is my idea, bearing in mind that we shall need the two fittest men in the party—that's you, Algy, and Bertie—to carry Henri. At twelve midnight Mario will drive Ginger and me to just this side of Monaco, to within reasonable walking distance of the harbour. It would be dangerous for him to go right into the town in case they are on the look-out for him. Our job will be to get the aircraft. Mario will return to Castillon, where Algy will be in charge. The whole party will get into the ambulance, which will then proceed to Cap Martin. Run along to the end of the cape and take cover in the trees, where the party will wait until François arrives with the boat. I shall arrange that with him. I gather he knows all about us, Bertie? Remember to tell me just where he lives.'

'Oh, yes, he knows all about you,' put in Bertie.

'Good. I shall ask him to try to be at the point of Cap Martin at two-thirty precisely. When he arrives, Algy's party will abandon the ambulance and go to the boat, taking with them Mario's spare can of petrol, and my uniform, which I shall need. Is that clear so far?'

'Perfectly clear,' confirmed Algy.

'The point about the can of petrol is this,' went on Biggles. 'François will come in under sail, and if he is all right for time he may not need the petrol. On the other hand, if there is a delay, the petrol can be used to speed things up. Put it in the tank, anyway. The boat will then proceed to a point about two miles off the tip of Cap Martin, where, if we are not there, it will wait. The time is now, shall we say, a few minutes to three, and the moon will be coming up. We shall aim to get away with the Savoia in order to arrive at the same time. In short, the rendezvous is two miles off Cap Martin at three o'clock. You'll probably have to use the engine to come alongside—if we try to come to you we may swamp you. Both parties will have to make every possible effort to be on time. I think that's all—except if the aircraft doesn't show up by three-fifteen you'll know we've come unstuck, in which case François will take you back to Cap Martin, from where Mario will drive you to Castillon. That's only in the event of failure. Should it happen, Algy, in charge of the party, will have to devise some other means of getting home. Is that all absolutely clear?'

'Yes, it seems perfectly straightforward,' agreed Algy. 'You've landed yourself, as usual, with the dirty end of the stick. Have you any idea of how you are going to get hold of this aircraft?'

'More or less. We shall simply swim out to it, cut the cable and start up. Whether we taxi to the rendezvous, or take off, will depend on the circumstances—it's only five or six miles from the harbour to Cap Martin. Looking at the thing now, there appears to be nothing to prevent anyone from doing that, but as a result of past experience we know jolly well that some snag usually turns up to upset things. Anyway, that's the scheme, and we shall stick to it as long as nothing occurs to bust it up.'

'Assuming that all goes according to plan, and we get the machine, where do you propose to make for?' asked Ginger.

'I shall try to run straight through to England. Naturally, that will depend on how much fuel we find in the tanks, and the wind, if any. I've left the wind out of my calculations because the weather seems settled.'

'What about Lucille?' asked Ginger. 'I've got very fond of that little moke.'

'Algy can turn her loose; she'll browse on these hills till someone picks her up. Maybe she'll find her way home. Any more questions?'

Nobody answered, so the plan, as outlined, was accepted. It was now late in the afternoon. The others were called up from the cellar and informed of the decision.

The princess smiled. 'But this is most romantic. My ancestors would be chuckling in their graves if they knew. Until recent times, for hundreds of years this sort of thing went on up and down the coast, fighting, rescues, princes at war with each other, and the Saracens making raids everywhere.' The princess sighed. 'What days they were.'

'We're not doing so badly ourselves,' Ginger pointed out, glancing at Jeanette.

The princess intercepted the glance and smiled. 'I think you are doing very well,' she observed. 'When the war is over you must visit my home near Palermo— that is if Jeanette will let you. The Sicilian girls are very good looking.'

Jeanette blushed. The princess laughed. Ginger grinned sheepishly. Bertie shook his head sadly.

Mario produced some food. Nobody asked where he had got it from, but it was a welcome diversion. After that they sat and discussed the plan in all its aspects while the sun went down in a blaze of gold and crimson behind the long arm of Cap d'Antibes, far to the west. Princess Marietta went back to the cellar and returned to say that Henri seemed slightly better. His mother was still with him.

'Which reminds me,' said Algy, addressing Biggles.

'Do you really feel up to this show to-night? You haven't been on your feet very long.'

'I couldn't do it if there was likely to be much violent exercise,' admitted Biggles. 'But as far as one can foresee, that isn't likely to arise. Bar accidents, I should be okay.'

Algy did not pursue the subject, and after that there was little to do except wait for the time to pass until zero hour.

Just before midnight, after a handshake all round, Biggles, Ginger and Mario, in accordance with the arrangement, went to the ambulance which, not without difficulty, was coaxed back to the road. At Biggles' suggestion they all sat on the front seat, where their uniforms would be seen if they were stopped, and so made their way, slowly, for the night was dark, to Mentone. Turning right, Mario went on to the outskirts of Monte Carlo, the ambulance taking its place in a considerable convoy going in the same direction. At a convenient spot it stopped. Biggles and Ginger got out. Mario turned the car and disappeared up the road on the return journey. Biggles and Ginger walked on towards the harbour. There were a number of Italian military cars, guns and tanks, parked beside the road, and a fair number of soldiers were moving about, but none had anything to say to the two officers who walked along as though they were out for a stroll before turning in. Without once being accosted they reached the harbour, where a few soldiers, presumably late arrivals, were having a midnight bathe. In a few minutes they were outside François' little house, knocking on the door.

It was opened after a short delay by the old boatman in his nightshirt. He looked startled when he saw his uniformed visitors, but Biggles soon put him at ease by explaining who they were. 'May we come in?' he concluded.

'*Oui, oui, messieurs*, enter,' invited François cordially.

They went in and closed the door.

In the tiny parlour Biggles explained why they had come to see him. 'I know that you will be willing to help us, because by helping us you will be helping France,' he went on. As he spoke Biggles took from his pocket his roll of French notes, and in spite of François' protests he pressed it into his hand. 'I can't take the money with me,' he pointed out. 'I shall have no means of carrying it in the water; if I tried it would only get wet, and spoiled.'

François demurred, but in the end accepted the money—a big sum for a man in his position.

Biggles then went on to describe just what he wanted him to do, that under the pretence of looking at his lobster pots he should sail along to Cap Martin, pick up the refugees, and take them to the rendezvous. Without hesitation François expressed his willingness to do this. He went quietly upstairs and returned fully dressed.

'I will go now,' he said.

'Yes, you had better start right away to be on the safe side,' agreed Biggles. 'Whatever happens, you must be at Cap Martin by half-past two.' He looked at his watch. 'You should manage it; there isn't much breeze, but you've got nearly two hours.'

'If the wind goes I use my oars,' said François.

'What about your wife? Is she awake? Does she know about this? I ask because we shall have to stay here for a while.'

'No, she sleeps,' answered François. 'It is better not to tell her. And so you will remain here?'

203

'Yes, if you don't mind,' replied Biggles. 'We had to come early in order to explain everything and give you a chance to get Cap Martin. We will just sit here quietly.'

'*C'est bon. Au revoir, messieurs.*' François departed.

'Now we've got to kill time,' Biggles told Ginger, standing where, through the open window, he could watch the harbour. It was too dark to see very much, but splashing indicated that some of the troops were still bathing. 'I hope they'll stay there,' went on Biggles, referring to the bathers. 'It will be supposed that we are in the party when we take to the water if we are seen. By the way, I propose to take the C.O.'s machine—it will probably be the best of the bunch. It means a swim of about a hundred yards. We'll land on the buoy, and pull the machine up to it.'

'What about these uniforms?'

'I was thinking about that. It's an awkward business swimming in clothes. I shan't need mine after I leave here because Algy is bringing my own uniform along. I can put it on later in the machine. What about you? If you leave your Italian outfit here, where are you going to wear later on?' Biggles smiled. 'You'll find it a bit parky, flying in your birthday suit!'

'You don't suppose I'm going to join the party looking like Adam, do you?' answered Ginger coldly. 'There are ladies, don't forget. I'll dump my tunic, but stick to the slacks, also my shirt. We shall have to abandon our shoes.'

Nothing more was said for a little while. Then Biggles remarked, 'This waiting is a tedious business, but it couldn't be avoided. Mario had to get back and we had to give François time to do his stuff.'

Not until twenty to three did Biggles move. Then he

stripped off his uniform, retaining only his vest, pants and belt. Through the belt he pushed his automatic, and a sheathed stiletto which he took from his pocket.

'Where on earth did you get that knife?' asked Ginger.

'Borrowed it from Mario.'

'What's the idea? Are you going to start stabbing people?'

'Not yet. It's to cut the mooring rope. We can't waste time untying wet knots. Got your gun?'

'It's in my trousers pocket. My torch is in the other if you need it.' As he spoke Ginger discarded his tunic and shoes.

'All right. Let's get along,' proposed Biggles. 'We'd better take these uniforms with us and dump them in the drink; it won't do to leave them here in case there's a row, and a search, in which case François would get it in the neck.'

Picking up the now unwanted clothes, they went out and closed the door softly behind them. One or two swimmers still lingered on the quay, otherwise the harbour was quiet. The water lay placid under the stars. Some distance out the silhouettes of the aircraft could just be seen, looking like prehistoric monsters tethered to rocks. Faintly across the water strains of music came from the customs house, where a radio was playing a waltz. Vague shadows could be seen moving against the light of a half-open door.

Biggles lowered himself gently into the water and jettisoned his uniform. Ginger did the same. Ripples spread from the spot, reflecting the cool light of the stars.

Without a word, using a steady breast stroke, they began swimming towards their objective.

Chapter 18

How the Rendezvous Was Kept

Nothing of interest occurred during the short swim, which was carried out with greater regard for quiet than for speed. Biggles and Ginger breasted the water together, leaving an ever-widening V to mark their passage across the tranquil face of the harbour. A silvery flush spreading upwards from beyond the distant Italian alps proclaiming the approach of the moon; reflected in the water, it caressed the ripples as they receded diagonally on either hand to lap at last against the quay.

Reaching their objective, they pulled themselves up on the rusty buoy to rest for a moment to listen, and wring the brine from their hair and eyes. Then Biggles grasped the mooring rope, and bracing himself, drew the big aircraft gently towards him. The rope coming within his reach, Ginger also pulled, hand over hand, until the cabin was level with the buoy.

'That's it, hold her,' breathed Biggles, and reached for the door.

As he did so a medley of sounds occurred on the shore. They began with a shout, which was followed by a number of short blasts on a whistle. Footsteps could be heard, running. Someone rapped out orders in brittle Italian.

Ginger looked with askance at Biggles. He could

think of only one reason for the alarm—that they had been seen. 'They've spotted us,' he said in a low voice.

Biggles looked around and then focussed his attention on the customs-house, where a number of men could be seen assembling as if for a parade. Lights appeared, both moving and stationary.

'No, it isn't us,' he said. 'Those fellows are not carrying rifles. It must be some sort of guard turn-out. Listen.'

Someone appeared to be shouting names. An order was given. The party turned to the right. Another order, and the men began marching along the Quai de Plaisance. By this time sounds of activity could also be heard on the Quai de Commerce opposite.

'I don't get it,' muttered Ginger. 'What is there on the Quai de Commerce?'

'Coal bunkers and gas-works mostly. It's the commercial side of the port. I don't know what's going on, but I don't think it has anything to do with us. Let's keep going. Give me your torch.'

Biggles opened the door of the aircraft and stepped inside. He switched on the torch, and deflecting the beam downwards, started to make a survey of the cabin. The light moved only a short way, then stopped.

Ginger, entering the aircraft behind Biggles, saw a sight both unexpected and disconcerting. Using an Italian Air Force tunic as a pillow, on a bunk lay a man, dressed in trousers and a shirt. He was awake. He had half raised himself on his elbow and was blinking into the glare. He had obviously been sleeping; awakened by the door being opened, he looked dazed at what must have seemed a strange intrusion. Suddenly he appeared to realize that he was in danger, for, letting out a yell, he started to get off the bunk.

Two swift strides took Biggles to him, gun in hand, whereupon the man, evidently a member of the crew, sat down again, stiff with fright.

Biggles tried him first in French, then in English, but the man apparently knew neither language. With a ghost of a smile he murmured to Ginger, 'Snag number one.'

'What are you going to do with him?'

'You keep an eye on him while I have a look at the cockpit,' answered Biggles. 'I shan't be a minute.' He went forward.

Ginger made signs to the Italian, by tapping his gun, that he would be wise to remain quiet. He could hear someone shouting, but who it was and what it was about he did not know.

Presently Biggles came back. 'I think everything's all right,' he said. 'We'd better get rid of this chap— we don't want any more passengers.' He looked at the Italian and indicated the door.

The man needed no second invitation. He was out like a shot, making for the shore at a fast overarm stroke. Biggles cut the cable. As he came back into the cabin and closed the door a searchlight was switched on. The beam did not fall on the aircraft, but swept across the water near the harbour mouth.

'It was that fellow shouting that did it,' muttered Ginger savagely.

'Possibly,' answered Biggles calmly. 'Come on, let's get away.' They went through to the cockpit and took their places.

When the twin engines came to life the noise, after the silence, was shattering. Biggles sat with one hand on the master throttle and the other on the control column, giving the motors a chance to warm up, until the searchlight swept back and came to rest on the machine, flooding it with radiance. Looking out of a side window, just beyond the beam, Ginger could see people running about on the quay.

'I think it's time we were moving,' he remarked. 'Our engines have sort of stirred things up.'

'I rather expected they would,' replied Biggles, smiling. 'Still, I don't think they dare to do much shooting here for fear of hitting the other machines. All the same, we'd better be getting along.'

He eased the throttle open. His face was expressionless as his eyes focused on the narrow harbour entrance beyond which lay the open sea. The flying-boat began to surge forward, increasing its speed as he advanced the throttle. Fifty yards from the harbour entrance it was skimming the water, flinging clouds of spray on either side.

'We've done it!' shouted Ginger triumphantly.

Biggles did not answer. His body suddenly went rigid. With a quick movement he leaned forward to bring his face nearer to the windscreen.

Dazzled by the light, which was playing on the side of the machine, for a moment Ginger could see nothing; then he made out a black bulk, seeming to fill the opening through which they must pass. He realized at once what it was. High masts left him in no doubt. A vessel of some sort was coming in. Instantly he understood the commotion on the quay. The ship had been signalled, and arrangements were being made for its reception. From their low position they had been unable to see it. He went cold with shock. In the tricky light he found it impossible to tell just how far away the ship actually was, but it looked horribly close.

Biggles thrust the throttle wide open. The engines

bellowed. Spray flew. The hull quivered. The aircraft tore on to what seemed certain destruction. Ginger sat still, petrified. There was nothing he could do. He stared at the black silhouette as though it had mesmerized him.

'Unexpected snag number two,' said Biggles, through set teeth.

Now it had seemed to Ginger, when he first saw the vessel, that it was actually coming into the harbour, but as the aircraft raced on he perceived that this was not the case. It was close, but, naturally, so near the harbour, it was travelling dead slow. The impression that it was travelling fast was created by the high speed of the aircraft, and as it turned out, the destroyer—as the vessel now revealed itself to be—was still a cable's length* from the entrance.

Biggles could not turn, of course, until he was out of the harbour, otherwise he must have collided with the sea wall. Neither could he take off, for the machine, running on a flat surface without a wave to give it a 'kick' into the air, was only just beginning to lift. He might have cut the throttle, in which case the machine would have slowed up, so that the force of impact, when the collision occurred, would have been trivial. But that would have ended any chance of escape. So he raced on, still on full throttle, and as he shot through the harbour mouth he kicked on full right rudder. There was nothing else for it, for by this time the black hull was towering above them. Even so, it was a desperate expedient. The aircraft yawed so violently that Ginger clutched at the side, thinking they were going right over. The port wing came down on the

*A distance of approximately 180 metres.

water with a smack, flinging up a cloud of spray that blotted everything from sight. He braced himself for the shock of collision which he still thought was unavoidable. Instead, the aircraft righted itself; the spray disappeared aft, and the machine, on a new course, shot past the destroyer with a few feet to spare.

He had another shock when he saw that there were three ships—two destroyers, and what he took to be a tanker. The fact that they were in line ahead had prevented the two rear vessels from being seen. For the same reason there was no risk of collision with them, for the aircraft was now travelling diagonally away from them. Ginger let out his pent-up breath with a gasp, but still he did not speak. A sidelong glance revealed Biggles still sitting as though nothing untoward had happened.

But the incident was not yet over. From the leading destroyer a searchlight stabbed the night. It found them at once. The shore searchlight joined in, and the aircraft, and the water round it, were transformed to polished silver. A moment later all vibration ceased, and Ginger knew they were airborne.

As the Savoia started to climb more searchlights thrust long white fingers into the starlit sky. Lines of tracer bullets* glittered in the beams. Bursting shells began to tear the sky with flame. Biggles pushed the control column forward for speed, and then zoomed high, leaving the searchlights below him. For a few minutes he flew on, turning first one way then another to mislead the gunners. Then, suddenly, he laughed aloud.

---

* Phosphorus-loaded bullets whose course through the air could be seen by day or by night.

'By gosh! I thought we were into that leading destroyer. We can't grumble, but it was foul luck. It shows how the best scheme can come unstuck—one can't make allowances for that sort of thing. Just imagine it. I don't think there has been a ship in that harbour for days, yet those blighters had to come in at the very moment we chose to go out. Had they been one minute earlier, or we a minute later, there would have been an almighty splash.'

'You're telling me,' muttered Ginger.

Biggles chuckled. 'I'll bet that skipper's using some language.'

'He was probably struck dumb, like I was,' growled Ginger. 'By the way, where are we going?'

'I'm trying to lead those sharpshooters to believe that we're heading out to sea,' returned Biggles. 'I daren't turn too soon or they'd know we were coming back. I think it's all right now.'

He turned in a wide half circle. The roar of the motors faded, and the flying boat settled down in a steady glide towards the nearest point of land—the tip of Cap Martin, now visible in the light of the moon some miles to the north. Ginger did not fail to notice the wisdom of Biggles's choice in the matter of time. They had worked under cover of darkness when they most needed it; now they had the light of the moon to enable them to pick up François' boat.

'Have you noticed the petrol gauges?' inquired Biggles.

Ginger admitted that he had not.

'Take a look.'

Not knowing quite what Biggles meant, but aware that there must be a reason for the remark, Ginger looked at the instrument panel. Then he understood. The tanks were less than quarter full.

'What a mob,' he muttered, in a voice heavy with disgust. 'Fancy being in port all that time and not filling up.'

'Perhaps they couldn't,' replied Biggles drily. 'Maybe it was because they were short of juice that they put in at Monaco. Since the machines were due to leave in the morning, obviously they were expecting to refuel before then. If that were so it would answer several questions. That was a tanker just gone in. I'd say that's what they were waiting for—hence the activity on the Quai de Commerce. It didn't occur to me to look to see if anything was coming, but the Italians were evidently expecting the ships. Not that it matters now. Can you see the boat?'

Away to the left searchlights were still quartering the sky, seeking the aircraft, but Ginger wasted no time on them. Concentrating his attention on the sea off Cap Martin he made out a small black speck.

'There she is!' he cried. 'They've made it.'

Biggles did not answer, but devoted himself to the difficult task of putting the flying-boat on the water in moonlight made deceptive by the waving arms of searchlights. Ginger said no more, knowing that it was no time for talking. He sat quite still, his eyes on the little boat that grew steadily larger and more definite in outline. Occasionally the water reflected a distant burst of flak, and he wondered vaguely what the Italians were shooting at. He had a curious sensation that this was not really happening—that he was watching a film.

They were now low enough for the shimmer on the water to break up into isolated ripples, and the conical

213

hills behind Cap Martin rose ever higher as the flying-boat continued to lose height. As it neared the sea its nose lifted a little, and then, as Biggles flattened out, François' boat was hidden behind the sweeping bows. There came a splash. Spray flew. Another splash that was drawn out into a long hiss. Powerful brakes seemed to hold the Savoia back. Rocking a little it came to rest.

'Get the door open,' ordered Biggles crisply. 'Ask Algy for my uniform—I'm none too warm.'

Ginger opened the door. A searchlight was groping dangerously close, and in the reflection of its light he saw the *Bluebird* skimming over the dancing ripples towards the machine, leaving a creamy wake to mark its course and reveal that it was running under power. It was about a hundred yards away.

Ginger waited, keeping an anxious eye on the quest-ing beams, some of which were now raking the water. He supposed that the machine had been picked up by the sound-detectors—or it might have been the throb of the *Bluebird*'s powerful engine.

The motor-boat surged alongside.

'Nice work,' called Algy.

'Nice work yourself,' answered Ginger. 'Make it snappy—we've sort of stirred up things where we've come from. If one of those beams hits us the Italians will start throwing things.'

Chapter 19
Farewell To France

As if to confirm Ginger's prediction a deflected beam swept over them, halted, came back, and then held them in a flood of blinding radiance.

'Biggles wants his kit!' shouted Ginger. 'He's flying in his pants.'

'Coming up.' Algy threw a bundle aboard, and Ginger, with a shout to Biggles, tossed it into the cabin.

The passengers followed. First, Henri was lifted in. He was followed by his mother, sister, and the princess. Biggles, who had managed to get into his slacks, appeared, calling for François.

'If you'll take my advice, François,' he said, as the others came aboard, 'you'll run that boat into Mentone. Say you were lobstering when the row started and you made for land to get out of the way. If they question you you can tell them that you saw a flying-boat pick up a party of people from Cap Martin. *Adieu.* I'll see that your good work is put on record.'

'Come back after the war!' shouted François. '*Au revoir. Au revoir*, milord, *et bon voyage**.' With its propeller churning, the motor-boat backed away, turned, and sped like an arrow towards the land.

As Ginger slammed the door a shell screamed over-head and flung up a plume of water a hundred yards beyond. He hurried through to the cockpit and saw

* French: Goodbye, My Lord, and have a good journey.

that Biggles was back in his seat. Glancing out of a side window he observed little tongues of fire spurting from the sombre mass of Mont Agel. More shells screamed.

'Let's get out of this,' he told Biggles.

The motors roared; the aircraft raced seaward, tearing a long white scar across the face of the water.

Ginger waited for the aircraft to lift before he spoke again. 'It's annoying to be so short of juice,' he remarked. 'Where are you making for?'

'Algeria.'

Ginger started. 'Strewth! Why Algeria?'

'Our chaps are there—or at least I hope they are. There's nowhere else within range of our petrol. I'm by no means sure that we shall get to Algeria, if it comes to that. If we make it, we ought to arrive about dawn. Take over while I get into my tunic.'

Biggles finished dressing.

'Okay,' he went on. 'Now go aft and warn Bertie and Algy to get in the gun turrets and keep an eye open for hostile aircraft—and by hostile I mean our own. We're flying under false colours, but our boys are not to know it.'

Ginger glanced through the window and saw that the rugged outline of the famous Azure Coast was already far behind. The searchlights were still waving, but they were mere matchstalks of light. He went back into the cabin and had a few words with the others, who had arranged themselves as comfortably as circumstances permitted. Mario, looking rather frightened, was squatting on the floor. Henri, pale but conscious, lay on the bunk. He was well enough to give Ginger a smile. Ginger received a similar greeting from Jeanette.

'Biggles wants you to man the turrets and watch for any of our lads who happen to be out looking for trouble,' he said, addressing Algy and Bertie.

'I say, that's a bit of a bore,' answered Bertie. 'By the way, why are we heading south? That isn't the way home.'

'It's the way we've got to go,' reported Ginger. 'We're short of juice. Biggles is making for the Algerian coast. He reckons we might just do it, but it's going to be a close thing. That's all. I'm going for'ard—see you later.' Ginger returned to the cockpit.

For more than two hours the Savoia roared its trackless way across a lonely moonlit sea. The islands of Corsica and Sardinia with their needle crags had long been left behind. No aircraft was seen. The only marine craft was a destroyer, or light cruiser, off the southwest coast of Sardinia.

'How about calling up our people on the radio and telling them we're on the way?' suggested Ginger once, in a moment of absent-mindedness.

'And call up a bunch of Italian fighters at the same time?' answered Biggles sarcastically. 'Leave it alone. I've had all the trouble I want for a little while.'

Biggles was now flying with one eye on the petrol gauge and the other on the southern horizon—so to speak. Fuel was getting low. At a quarter to six a pink glow in the east heralded the approach of another day, and when, a few minutes later, a purple smudge materialized across the horizon Biggles announced his relief.

'Just in time,' he observed. 'We're down to our last pint. Keep your eyes skinned. Our only danger now is from our own aircraft.'

'That would be a pity,' murmured Ginger.

217

In ten minutes, under a sky aflame with colour and the disc of the sun coming up like a enormous toy balloon, the smudge had crystallized into a sandy coastline backed by sloping cliffs whose faces had been scarred and grooved by centuries of sun and wind and rain. The land ran east and west until it finally merged into the indefinite distance.

'Africa,' said Ginger quietly.

'Algeria—I hope,' rejoined Biggles. 'This is where we shall have to watch our step.'

Hardly had the words left his lips when the port motor choked; the other did the same, and after a few backfires they both cut out dead. By that time Biggles had pushed the control column forward, putting the aircraft into a shallow glide towards the land.

'We shall just about do it,' he observed.

Bertie appeared. 'I say, chaps, get a move on,' he requested. 'There are three Hurricanes coming up astern.' As he spoke, from somewhere not far away came the snarling grunt of multiple machine guns.

Biggles threw the Savoia into a steep sideslip. To Bertie he shouted, 'Get out on the hull and put your hands up!'

Ginger looked down at a sea where white-capped breakers were flinging themselves on a foam-fringed beach. 'You'll never get down there,' he asserted.

'I've got to,' answered Biggles grimly.

'She'll swamp.'

'I intend her to—in shallow water,' said Biggles crisply. 'I'm afraid if we did manage to land our lads would shoot us up. I'm going to try to run in with the surf and beach her. There's nothing else for it. You'd better get aft and warn everybody to be ready for a crash-landing. You and Algy stand by Henri.'

Ginger went aft—no easy matter considering the angle of the aircraft—to find Bertie in the main gun-turret making frantic signals to the pursuing pilots, who were probably finding it difficult to bring their sights to bear on a target which, as Biggles intended by his sideslip, was travelling on a deceptive course.

'It'll be all right,' announced Ginger, with a confidence he certainly did not feel. 'We may have to crash-land on the sand. Be ready to get out quickly.' He caught Jeanette's eyes and smiled encouragement, and then clutched at a seat as the aircraft came to even keel. Through a window he could see breakers curling for their rush at the beach. The aircraft was travelling in the same direction. Then spray blotted out the scene.

The machine raced on, overtaking waves that slapped like giant clappers at the skimming keel. Then came a shuddering jar that flung everybody forward. The door burst open. Water poured in and swirled along the floor. Shingle pattered like hail. With a final crash the aircraft came to rest, listing a little to one side.

Sliding to the door Ginger saw that they were on the beach, on the fringe of the sea where lacy foam made scalloped patterns on the sand. Somewhere near an engine howled. 'Look after Henri!' he shouted, and running up the shelving beach lifted his arms as a sign of surrender. He was just in time. A diving Hurricane lifted its nose, and instead of firing, as had clearly been the pilot's intention, zoomed high. For an instant the noise of its motor drowned all other sounds. All three Hurricanes went into a tight circle over the flying-boat.

Ginger turned to find Bertie and Algy coming ashore with Henri, and the others following. Biggles brought up the rear. Walking up the dry sand they stood in a little group. Biggles waved to the Hurricanes, and then, with the broad side of an oyster shell, wrote in huge letters on the smooth wet sand, the one word, 'British'. A Hurricane came in low, wing down, and then, banking steeply, raced along the beach towards the west.

'Do you know where we are?' Ginger asked Biggles.

'Not exactly, but I reckon we're somewhere east of Algiers,' answered Biggles. 'That looks like a vehicle coming along the coast road. Perhaps the driver will give us our position. Let's go up.'

As it happened there was no need for them to go to the road for the vehicle turned out to be an American jeep filled with troops.

Biggles stopped, smiling. 'Looks like the Yanks are coming,' he observed. 'They've spotted us.'

The jeep stopped with a jerk. The troops jumped out, and with rifles and Tommy guns* advanced suspiciously, a sergeant ahead of the rest.

'Okay, boys,' called Biggles, 'we're friends.'

'What goes on here?' growled the sergeant, after a glance at the Italian aircraft. 'Who are you?'

'I'm Squadron Leader Bigglesworth, of the British Royal Air Force,' Biggles told him.

The sergeant looked puzzled. 'What are you doing with that ship?'

'We borrowed it from the Italians to get across the ditch,' returned Biggles. 'We've come from France. I've got a sick man here, and there are ladies in the party, so I'd be obliged if you'd give us a lift to your headquarters. I've got to get in touch with a senior air officer as quickly as possible.'

* A sub-machine gun, the original designed by Thompson, used by the American troops.

'Okay British, get aboard,' invited the sergeant. 'We haven't far to go.'

That, really, is the end of the story, for the rest was mere routine. Having explained the position to the officer in charge of the American landing party, after Henri had received medical attention and the others some light refreshments, the refugees were taken by road to British headquarters, in Algiers, where they were made comfortable. The A.O.C. sent a signal to the Air Ministry reporting their arrival. Henri was taken to hospital.

After that they spent a week in Algiers waiting for transport home—a period that was all too short for Ginger, who spent most of his time walking and swimming with Jeanette. At the end of the week they were flown to England in a homeward-bound troop-carrier. After seeing their overseas visitors comfortably settled the officers reported to Air Commodore Raymond of the Air Ministry, who congratulated them on the successful outcome of their mission.

'Well, that's that,' remarked Biggles, after they had completed their reports and went out into Kingsway. 'I suppose we might as well get back to the squadron.'

'I've got a spot of leave to finish, if you don't mind, sir,' said Ginger meekly.

Biggles raised his eyebrows. 'What do you want leave for?'

'Well, I've got to see my tailors about a new uniform—and one or two other things,' explained Ginger, in an offhand way.

Biggles smiled. Algy shook his head sadly. Bertie winked.

221

'Give her my love, and all that sort of rot—if you see what I mean?'

'You run away and polish your eyeglass, troubadour,' sneered Ginger, and hailed a passing taxi.